SEX, DEATH, & HONEY

The Misadventures of Butch Quick, Book 1

BRIAN KNIGHT

Tulpa Books

ALSO BY BRIAN KNIGHT

Horror - Novels

- Feral
- Broken Angel
- Hacks

Horror - Omnibus

- They Call Us Monsters

Horror - Chapbooks

- Children of Filth
- Heart of the Monster
- Apocalypse Green
- Johnny Junk
- Death is Blind
- Midnight Blues
- The Beast Inside - The Berserkers, Part 1
- Blood Rage - The Berserkers, Part 2

Horror - Collections

- Dragonfly

The Phoenix Girls - Fantasy

- The Conjuring Glass (Book 1)
- The Crimson Brand (Book 2)
- The Heart of the Phoenix (Book 3)

The Misadventures of Butch Quick - Crime

- A Face Full of Ugly - A Chapbook
- Big Trouble in Little Boots - A Chapbook
- Sex, Death, and Honey (Book 1)

For my Honey, Shawna Knight. Thank you for everything.

INTRODUCTION BY ED GORMAN

"There are advantages to being a seven-foot tall, two-hundred-and-fifty pound Indian with a face like a leather football helmet, but this wasn't one of them." - Butch Quick

I need to start this with a story of my own. Several years ago I was hired to ghost a book about bounty hunters. The everyday kind. Not the Dog ones or any of the other melodramatic kind. The ones whose big signs you pass by in the area near the city and/or county lock ups. Regular folk in other words.

The celebrity I was working with had a show that went in the tank so the project was scrapped. But since I'd spent two months interviewing twenty-some bounty hunters about their jobs I had a decent idea about how they functioned in the world. Some surprises: A good share of bounty hunters are women. Male and female bounty hunters alike tend to ask the police to go along if they think there's going to be trouble. Bounty hunters rely on computers even more than hackers and writers. Yes there's always the prospect of danger but unless you're involved in a reality show you try to hold it to a minimum.

Right off I liked Brian Knight's version of a bounty hunter because it seemed realistic.

The other thing I liked, the thing that made this unique and fascinating story even better, was the voice. We read different books for different reasons. There are writers I read for plot. Their characters never strike me as more than spear carriers and there's never much wit or insight in the psychology but by God I'm up till three a.m. turning those pages. Then there are writers I read for the way they present and understand their characters. Their plots may not dazzle me that much but I'm hooked on the human drama. And then there's voice. To me this is the rarest of all writerly gifts.

All you have to read are two or three paragraphs and you know you're reading Elmore Leonard. Or Ray Bradbury. Or Lucius Shepard. Brian Knight is young, but with Sex, Death & Honey he's developing a voice all his own. For me the first person voice lends itself to a kind of ongoing confession. "I" narrative is filled with opinions whether the writer always intends them or not. And in opinions are truths about how the protagonist (and likely the writer) feels about the world he's presenting.

I liked this book a great deal. I will now make sure to read everything else Brian Knight publishes if that tells you anything.

Oh—and the story itself. Funny thing. Every time I synopsize a book or movie on my blog readers bitch about how lame I am at boiling things down.

So let me say that Mr. Knight presents a) a plot that

will keep you up late at night b) insights into various kinds of life that are rich with wisdom and wit, and c) and a voice you'll remember for a long, long time to come.

Enjoy.

Ed Gorman,

January 2012

CHAPTER 1

This is Paradise Valley.

The city sits cradled in a valley at the furthest western foot of the Rocky Mountains. Two rivers run through it, the Snake River from south to north, the Clearwater River from east to west, and meet at the port district. Its major exports are paper, lumber, and grain. Its major imports are drugs and pain.

Paradise Valley is also a tourist hot spot. We have the gateway to Hells Canyon, America's deepest river gorge, and the Nez Perce Indian Casino a few miles east just across the Idaho border.

One hundred thousand souls give or take, roughly half of them either lost or getting there. We have meth and marijuana, hookers and pimps, bums and burnouts, and a per capita murder rate that makes our local politicians blush. We don't have mimes and street performers, the pushers and pimps won't tolerate that caliber of scum, so it's not all bad I suppose.

East Paradise Valley, the half of our city east of the

Snake River, is the better half, almost respectable. West Paradise Valley . . . not so much.

Hang with me for a while and I'll show you a side to this city that you won't find on the Chamber of Commerce website.

Welcome to Paradise.

The West Valley Friday Street Fair was like a low rent Mardi Gras with a family friendly veneer so thin it was almost transparent. On top there were the pretzel and hot dog stands, the coffee bar, even the beer garden tucked back behind Station 3, and every other business along Main Street with a booth or display set up on sidewalks or in the middle of the road. The city closed off four blocks of Main Street every Friday afternoon from Easter to Halloween, and it seemed half the city turned out. There were also pushers, pickpockets, and other assorted lowlife present. This was their half of the city after all. It would be rude not to invite them.

I never had much to do with the street fair. Too many damned people for my liking, and there was never anything there I was particularly interested in.

That late September evening was an exception to the general rule. There was something there that day I was very interested in, and after only a half-hour of ignoring the vendors and dodging hyperactive kids on the peaks of sugar highs, I found her.

Kecia Wilson.

Dark-haired and pale-skinned, slim and short, she looked like a young librarian in her horn-rimmed glasses. I spotted her loitering in a graveled square between buildings usually reserved for Elks Lodge parking. That day there were no cars, just two rows of Porta Potties, six in a row lined up against the sides of the buildings, arranged by the city for its citizens' shitting convenience.

I slipped into the recessed entrance of a closed insurance office and watched as dusk deepened.

Foot traffic in and out of shit-house square was sparse and fluid, never more than a handful at a time and never for longer than it took to do their business and sanitize their hands.

Except for Kecia.

Kecia stayed on the move, never stood in one place for more than a minute, but never left the square. Like she was waiting for someone.

I was counting on that.

Kecia wasn't the person I was after that day. My night's target was a glowing example of West Paradise Valley street-shit named Phil Shepard. Kecia Wilson was a girlfriend and likely partner in crime, but I didn't have any business with her. My business was with Phil.

A skinny young skunk of a man emerged from a crowd around a tattoo booth, leaving a swath of turned heads and grimaces in his wake, and jittered his way over to her. A few moments of conversation, then she nodded curtly toward the second to last stall on the left and turned her back on him.

I watched, waited.

The young tweaker jittered his way over to the stall, hesitated, knocked.

The door opened a crack, and a few seconds later a

little more. Enough to see the man inside, his face half illuminated by the flickering glow of streetlamps.

Phil Shepard.

Jackpot!

A hand slid out, rubbed palms with the tweaker standing outside, a quick exchange, meth for cash, then withdrew.

I waited for the tweaker to clear out, then crossed the road.

A kid with a plush top hat and a cotton candy ran into me and bounced backward, falling on his ass. His carnival top hat went askew and his cotton candy hit the pavement to be trampled a moment later.

"Watch where you're going you big turd!"

The boy dusted himself off and glared at me before pounding away.

Heads turned to regard me with disapproval and disgust, Kecia among them.

Shit!

There are advantages to being a seven-foot tall, two-hundred-and-fifty pound Indian with a face like a leather football helmet, but this wasn't one of them. Once someone noticed me, they usually kept noticing me.

Kecia marked my approach with suspicion, and gasped when I stopped and turned to face her.

"Whatchu lookin' at, dickhead?" She stared up into my face from her not quite five foot vantage point, held her ground but remained ready to bolt at the slightest provocation.

I lifted the hem of my shirt, uncovered my badge and cuffs. This move also exposed a bulge in my front pocket;

my insurance against the unexpected in what can sometimes be a rough-and-tumble profession.

Kecia's eyes darted from badge to cuffs to bulge, and widened in alarm.

When a young woman sees a bulge in a man's pants, the Ruger LC9 is not the kind of 'Pocket Pistol' that leaps immediately to her mind, but I just let them think whatever the hell they want. The Ruger LC9 is a tiny little gun, it looked like a toy pistol in my hand. Flashing it would be more likely to elicit laughter than respect, so I leave it in its pocket holster unless I need to use it.

I've never tried to be Dirty Harry. I'd rather people didn't know I'm packing until my handy little Ruger is pointed at their nose. It looks a little less like a toy from that perspective.

"Move along please," I said, as pleasantly as I could.

She moved along, and quickly.

I watched until she was lost in the crowd, then proceeded to the magic stall.

I knocked.

"What's the word, amigo?" His voice was muffled behind the closed stall door.

Word?

So that was his girlfriend's job, to screen the legitimate customers from those who just needed to have a shit. The stall door was locked from the inside, no way to get at him unless he opened it.

I didn't have the *word*, so I knocked again.

"Ocupado, asshole!"

I knocked again.

"I said go shit somewhere else!"

I knocked again. I could keep this up all night if I needed to.

"Fuck!"

The *Occupied* sign slid to *Open* and the door followed suit.

"*You little . . .*" He stopped in mid-scream, then tilted his face up to mine.

I grabbed the door before he could pull it closed. He knew who I was, my face is hard to forget, but I spoke the words anyway. That's just the way it's done.

"Eagle Eye Bail Bonds."

He moved forward as if to run for it, and I shifted myself in front of him. For a second I thought he was going try to fight his way out, but he seemed to think better of it. People almost always panic when they realize they've been caught, and in those moments I find being large and scary looking very much to my advantage.

"You missed your court date," I said. "I gotta take you back in."

He smiled, nodded. "I figured you'd come looking for me."

He released the door and raised his arms to me, wrists close together and ready for the cuffs.

I relaxed. He was going to come quietly. I like it when things go smoothly.

His grin stretched to the edges of his acne-pitted face.

I realized belatedly that I had fucked up.

I've never been bitten in the ass by an electric eel, but if I ever am I have a good idea of what to expect.

I was reaching for my cuffs and keeping both eyes on Phil's grinning face when Kecia hit me from behind with the juice. The next several seconds were lost in a blaze of white-hot pain originating in my right ass-cheek and filling my whole body. My arms snapped down to my sides and my jaw slammed shut. My spine did a musical kind of snap, crackle and pop as it stiffened.

Phil's smug smile faded in a wash of white light.

And when I could see again I was laying in the gravel in front of the abandoned shitter, watching Phil and Kecia run toward the crowded street.

"Ditch that," Phil shouted, and snatched a short yellow wand from Kecia's hand, tossed it between the last two stalls before dragging her into the crowd. Seconds later they were gone, and I was left alone and twitching on the ground.

The party on Main Street continued unabated, only the occasional bored pedestrian glancing my way.

Someone passed me on the right, and another stepped over me on their way to Phil's abandoned stall, snickering.

Later, thirty seconds or thirty minutes maybe, all I knew for sure is that it was darker, I regained the use of my body and removed it from shit-house square. I paused only to retrieve Kecia's Wasp from where Phil had ditched it. It was a handy little thing. Under a foot long and packing somewhere around 5,000 volts. She'd probably kept it in her bag for just such an occasion.

I decided to hold on to it, maybe for the next time I ran into Phil Shepard and his girlfriend.

CHAPTER 2

The lady, Rita, was old beyond her years, fifty going on seventy, her face leathery and wrinkled, riddled with moles and skin tags. She had a respectable set of mutton-chop sideburns, cigarette-stained false teeth, and the phlegmy, bullfrog voice of a longtime smoker.

Her neighbor, Cameron Finke, was an inconsiderate fuckwad, the useless second-generation spawn of a local fat cat. He had a rock band and about a dozen little groupies. They would start tuning up at around nine every evening, and continue to tune up until inebriation or sexual exhaustion shut them down. They were experienced partiers, and blessed with the stamina of the young, so these party/jam sessions usually lasted until the early hours of the morning. Sometimes the band progressed past the tuning up and ventured into the playing of actual songs, a lot of eighties and nineties heavy metal mostly, but to call these songs covers would be an insult to cover bands around the world. They were more like parodies.

Finke held these nightly sessions in a renovated shop accessible by a narrow alley that passed between his square of property and the parking lot of the adjacent mini-mall. My one quick glance through the shop's open bay door the previous evening revealed a drum kit and various instruments on pedestals, a mini-bar and fridge, and a row of thrift shop sofas.

I knew enough about the guy to be wary of him; a minor drug bust across the state line in Idaho, rumors about a little moonlighting in the meth trade. Your basic West Valley street trash, but with a little more 'fuck you' money than most.

My name is Butch Quick, and I have been called many things, including an inconsiderate fuckwad. I am the mostly useless nephew of another local rich guy. Like Finke, I'm on the payroll of my wealthy relative. Unlike Finke, I don't have a garage band. My Uncle's business interests include Higheagle Classic Cars, Eagle Eye Bail Bonds, and Boomtown, a drinking establishment that passed for a nightclub only because of its lack of competition. Boomtown was the only place *in* town that hadn't given in to the new country music trend. It has live music every night, mostly unknown local bands, but every now and then he scored some real talent. Quiet Riot, John Fogerty, and Joan Jett have played there.

Depending on Uncle Higheagle's current needs I am a repo man, bouncer, bounty hunter, or parts runner. I have no preference; mostly it all pays the same.

Finke manages real estate for his grandpa; a few run down duplex apartments, half a dozen lots between his house and Elm Street, and the mini-mall next to it. The mini-mall boasted a thrift store, a liquor store, the local

DMV office, and a large empty space that used to house The Great Wall, an all-you-can-eat Chinese Buffet.

Rita claimed to have lost half of her cats after The Great Wall opened. Having eaten there once myself, I had some sympathy for her claim.

The reason for my interest in Cameron Finke, a 1968 Mustang convertible, was not currently at the property, and having nothing else to do I sat down for a *beverage* and a smoke with the chatty Rita. She was willing to talk, not because she particularly liked me, but because she sensed a way to screw over the neighbor from hell. She was also several *beverages* into the day and in a very sharing mood.

". . . and I just know they're smoking dope over there." She made a sound in her throat that I think was supposed to convey disgust. What the sound did convey was a great wad of snot, which she spat to the side of the small glass top lawn table we shared. "I can smell it across the street!"

She shook her fist at the innocuous little house across the street from us and made the phlegmy sound again.

The house was small, white, with a well-maintained square of grass in front and a row of neatly trimmed shrubs along the alley. From the outside the shop looked as average as the house, no sign of the redneck discotech housed inside. Between the two buildings was a slightly larger square of lawn than that up front, fenced, with a Beware of Dog sign.

It was an unassuming place; you almost expected to see a little old lady weeding her garden on the other side of the backyard fence, or a hunched old fella puttering outside the shop.

At the moment there was only Finke's Rottweiler stalking the fence line.

". . . called the cops and the big dumb-shits stopped here with their lights flashing . . ."

"Is he usually gone all day?" She had arrived back where our conversation had started a half-hour earlier. I decided if I was going to get down to the shit that mattered I'd have to be more aggressive. I was still aching a bit from the night before, not at my most sociable.

She looked incensed, and I thought *here's a woman used to having her say all the way to the end*. After a few seconds she seemed to decide to let it slide.

"Not always." She shrugged, made her deep throat sound, sipped her beverage. She lit a cigarette, slipped into a morose silence, gave me a reproachful look, clearly meant to imply her displeasure at being interrupted.

The silent treatment, I thought, and couldn't help a smile. "Thanks," I said, pushing up from her proffered lawn chair before she decided to forgive me. "I've gotta run."

She rose across from me, fumbling her drink back onto the glass-top table, nearly spilling it. "But you didn't tell me what's he's in trouble for."

"Nothing big," I said, and felt bad as her excitement ebbed. Truth is I kinda liked the old lady. I sympathized with her too I've had my share of shithead neighbors.

"Don't worry," I assured her. "It's still going to sting him plenty."

I could feel her eyes on me as I walked away, crossing the street in hurried strides to avoid the city's rambunctious traffic. To West Paradise Valley drivers, pedestrian right-of-way was more a suggestion than a rule. If they caught you outside a marked crosswalk you were fair game. My old Ventura, more balls than style but it got me from A to B, was parked in front of the liquor store. I pulled in facing away from the picture window displays, Four Loco, cheap wine, Jack Daniels, but got an eyeful on my way back. Four years on this side of my last drink, and stopping at my car instead of continuing on toward the flashing neon lights and hedonistic lure of the place was almost easy.

Inside the Ventura and facing safely away from temptation, I started the motor, cranked up the AC, turned the radio on, then up. The Doors . . . L.A. Woman. Nice.

I lit a cigarette, cracked my window enough to let the smoke blow out, watched Finke's house.

The Rottweiler continued its lonely and aggressive patrol, nearly shitting itself in its excitement to get at a passing kid.

Fifteen minutes passed. Finke stayed gone.

Time to head home.

Rita waved, then mimicked firing a gun toward Finke's house and winked as I drove by. I winked and waved back.

Often when I'm interviewing people they assume I'm a collector for the Tribal Casino tracking down unpaid markers or hunting for cheats and crooks. I've never seen fit to correct them. It gives me an air of intimidation and adds a bit of spice to their day. The tribal part I get, I don't live on the reservation but as far as most people are concerned an Indian is an Indian. I've stepped foot in the casino exactly once . . . the gift shop, to buy a souvenir hat.

I wear it when I'm interviewing people like Rita. It helps *encourage* the wrong assumption. The Tribal Casino doesn't actually employ *collectors*. No one gets in deep enough with them to warrant it. It's small-time, pay as you play. This is Washington State, not Vegas.

So far the only thing I'd learned about Finke's schedule was that he didn't have one. Sometimes he spent the entire day out of his house, sometimes he barely ventured outside it. When he did leave, it might be for hours, or only minutes. Sometimes he was alone, but most often not. His entourage was dynamic, changing almost day to day with only a few exceptions, the tattoo guy, who played guitar for his crappy little garage band, and the body builder, the guy who grunted and barked out lyrics. The position of bassist was as dynamic as the rest of his entourage, the current one a kid who lived in one of Cameron's properties. Rita said the kid usually left early.

Finke was a drummer.

The only time I could absolutely count on him being home was during the nightly party, which seemed to be impervious to angry neighbors and visits from the police, and in the early hours of the morning while he slept off the nightly party. Since I didn't expect Finke to be over-joyed about me taking back his big horsepower toy—they hardly ever were—I decided to wait until the post-party crash to cancel his contract with Uncle Higheagle. The getup in his shop was encouraging. He probably kept the Mustang parked outside, which meant it was mine for the taking.

Whatever debts Cameron Finke had incurred or laws he might have broken were not my concern. The only thing that mattered to me was the contract he'd broken with my uncle and the red Mustang he'd stopped paying for. One way or another that car was coming back with me.

A standard midnight grab, then home free.

Yeah, that's what I thought.

CHAPTER 3

Home was a small one-roomer near the port, larger than your average jail cell, but not a lot. It had a minuscule kitchen and a single enclosed rectangle of a bathroom with toilet, sink, and shower stall. In the rental market such units are called cabins, though this one had none of the homey, nostalgic appeal associated with the name. This is one of a dozen on Fair Street. The cabins were white, shabby, squatting between a gun repair shop on the Twelfth Street intersection and a flea market on the intersection of Thirteenth.

Mine was indistinguishable from the others on the outside, rundown on the inside. Dark wood panel walls, a mint-green linoleum floor that might have been installed about the time disco was born. No TV or radio, no pictures on the walls. The only photograph I owned lay face down on top of my small dresser. I kept it because I had to, but it had been a long time since I'd been able to look at the faces in it.

I am the only longtime resident of this stretch of West

Paradise Valley skid row. It was my rock bottom, almost five years ago, and I've never felt the need to move on. The usual tenants are kids working their way up, or addicts and tough luck cases working their way down. The occasional drifter drops anchor here as well, usually to cool his or her heels for a few weeks before moving on to wherever.

I try to meet them all at least once, but only in passing, *never* more than that. I don't make friends with them. We trade a few words, if they're the sort of folks capable of idle chat. I get a feel for them, then leave them alone. I am not a naturally sociable fellow, or a naturally curious one, but I like to know who I'm bunking down next to. I like to know who to watch out for.

I've shared my neighborhood with junkies and alkies, crack whores, crazies, newly single women and young men who would live in a box if it meant breaking loose from parental tyranny. I spent a month with a serial killer for a next-door neighbor, but that kind of thing happens in the best of neighborhoods.

I checked my answering machine, found one message from Uncle Higheagle. The Washington State Police were auctioning off impounded vehicles in Spokane that coming weekend. We'd Greyhound it up together and drive back with new stock for his lot. Nothing about my fuckup the night before, which was good for both of us. Good for me because dwelling on the past is bad for one's spiritual and mental health. I know this because shrinks have told me so. Good for Uncle Higheagle because his ability to overlook my fuckups saved him frequent disappointment.

I armed the security system, checked the clip and

safety on my bedside piece, the latest model CZ 75 9mm, the rail-mounted light and laser sight as much for intimidation as accuracy. I didn't have much of value in my cabin but I still valued my life enough to want to hold on to it a while longer.

I don't find guns to be attractive objects, but I own a few and I shoot well. Lots of practice and a bit of training with my old gun-nut friend Posey. Posey loved guns the same way a satyr loves women, many and often, and whenever possible, publicly. He's a state approved instructor, has won all the local shooter's competitions so often that organizers opted to recruit him as a judge as a way to bar him from competition.

Posey picked all my guns and related accessories for me. The compact Ruger LC9 and pocket holster for discrete protection on the job, the CZ 75 with its flashy accessories for home protection.

I slid my home protection beneath my pillow, set the alarm clock for a nine pm wake up, and lay in bed.

I did not sleep right away, I never did.

After a while I gave into restlessness and decided to read for a while. Reading in bed was the only sure way to put myself to sleep. It was better than Benadryl. I slid the drawer of my little bedside desk open and pulled out the black portfolio. I propped myself up in bed and unzipped it. Inside were a half-dozen photocopied police reports, nearly one hundred crime scene photos separated by case and tucked into snug plastic pockets, and my own extensive handwritten notes.

I was not supposed to have these, but I have a friend in the local FBI office and when the feds took over the Redwolf case she made sure I got copies. Her name was all over my notes, and she was the subject of one of the files. Gina White one of the toughest women I've ever known, a good friend to have.

Gina had gone through hell and come back alive. She understood

I ignored the photos, the images were tattooed on my aching brain and I didn't need to look at them, and read my notes for the thousandth time. It had been a long time since anything new went into my copy of the Redwolf files and I had most of the material committed to memory, but I read anyway.

While I read my body relaxed, trying to forget the minor indignities of the past few days and the major dishonors of a lifetime. My mind wandered and eventually shut down.

I dreamed about the first man I'd ever killed.

I remember the car, a late '90s Chrysler Neon, bad lines, no style. Not the kind of car I enjoyed driving, but I thought I was going to enjoy crashing it. It was my wife's car, but she wasn't going to need it anymore.

My passenger was a little man, bald, unimpressive on the surface, but beneath, something else. Roy Dickie. He wasn't aware of our destination, but was still less than enthusiastic about the journey. He didn't know the specifics, but got the general idea.

It wasn't good.

"Who are you?" He'd pressed himself back into the passenger seat, as if he hoped to escape me through it. "What do you want?"

I said nothing, just put the gas pedal down a little harder. We were on the highway by the river, two lanes of twisting blacktop with little margin for error. The speed limit on that stretch just outside of Paradise Valley was sixty. I had it up to eighty-five, and climbing . . . but slowly. No style or balls, that car.

I was a fraction of a second slow on the next sharp bend and slid, tires squealing, passenger squealing as well, into the oncoming lane. For a moment I thought the ride was over. So did my passenger. The sudden, sour stench of piss filled the cab. When I was back in my lane and in control again I popped the center console open, found the little travel-size aerosol can, sprayed the little man beginning to blubber in the passenger seat.

New Car Scent, a mix of fresh upholstery and Armor All.

"Why are you doing thi-his?" He shouted, his voice breaking into fresh sobs on the last word. The sound of his blubbering made me angry.

The car wandered dangerously again as I reached for him, cupped the back of his head in my right hand and brought it down hard against the dash. The padded plastic split beneath his head. I hoped for a cry of pain, a satisfying splash of blood, but the inconsiderate bastard passed out cold.

I slowed to a sane sixty and a minute later pulled into a deserted rest area.

He needed to be awake for what was coming next.

It was important.

He wasn't out for long, maybe another fifteen minutes, and as soon as he stirred I pulled back onto the highway, this time driving east toward the city.

"Wakey-wakey," I said when his eyes fluttered open and he lifted his head again. There was a little blood I was pleased to see, just a trickle from the splitting skin stretched over a rising goose egg on his forehead. "Can we start over without all the crying?"

It appeared he could. I was grateful for that at least.

"Why are you doing this?"

"For Daphne and Beth Quick," I said, and that was all.

I stomped the gas pedal down to the floor again, and I could feel myself grinning, inexplicably happy as the needle slowly climbed to illegal and dangerous speeds. Roy began to scream again, and I started to laugh. I couldn't help it.

The needle hovered just below ninety, the road made a sharp left turn.

I turned right instead.

I think he must have figured it out at the last second because he lunged for the steering wheel.

But it was already too late.

The alarm went off and I woke with my customary good grace, reaching for the gun beneath my pillow before thinking better of it and settling for thumping the snooze button with more force than was strictly necessary. I went through a lot of alarm clocks.

I surrendered to reality. Got up, pissed, drank coffee, went to work. I had a Mustang to rescue.

CHAPTER 4

I drove the old Ventura to a twenty-four hour grocery store a few blocks down from Cameron Finke's place and walked the rest of the way. By the time I reached Diagonal Street, the main drag that separated the industrial and commercial zoned blocks from the residential on that side of town, I could hear Finke's party winding up. I kept a distance, approaching only as close as the parking lot of the mini-mall's defunct Chinese Buffet, then turned east and walked to the little park near the bridge into East Paradise Valley.

I sat at the bench furthest from the road and watched the moon's reflection move across the surface of the Snake River's sluggish water, smoking my way through a pack of Camel Wides as the night ticked on.

Two blocks over the party continued. If Finke's band ever progressed past the tune-up phase, I couldn't tell. Don't get me wrong, I love good rock music, but what Finke's bunch produced couldn't be called good, nor music for that matter. The drone of loud chatter and laughter challenged it, but was not kind enough to overcome it.

I smoked, waited, checked the time on my cell phone. Twice cop cars passed by on patrol, the second stopping to shine a spotlight at me. I waved and it moved along. Neither car detoured toward the sound of the festivities at Finke's.

I dozed sometime past midnight, and awoke to the sound of 225 horses laying rubber on blacktop. A drunken female cheer rose up to encourage, and a second brief chirping of tires brought laughter.

I had no way of knowing it was the Mustang, but it was, and I did know it. On the whole I think Mustangs are overrated, but dammit I loved that car.

I rose from the bench, knees popping and legs stiff from my long sit-down, and walked toward Finke's. It was time to have a little look.

It *was* the Mustang, but by the time I had them in sight, still almost a block away but with a clear view across the mini-mall's rear parking area, the showboating was over. The party appeared to be over too.

Some of Finke's entourage left on foot, stumbling up or down Third Street, one crossed the empty parking lot in my direction, and others slumped behind the wheels of their cars and pickups. Finke was backing the Mustang into his shop, the tattoo guy and body builder standing to either side of the open bay like guards. The moment the

Mustang's front bumper cleared the door the two stepped inside and the door descended.

That was the first kink in my night's plans. Aside from the potential legal problems associated with breaking and entering, which I am not allowed to do, extracting a car from an ex-customer's locked garage is a logistical nightmare.

I started walking again, and the drunk who had set out in my direction continued stumbling toward me. I moved down Second Street away from Finke's house at a leisurely pace and pretended not to notice as Finke's friend turned the corner around the rear of the mini-mall and fell in behind me, only a quarter of a block away.

I don't like being followed. It makes me nervous. Especially when I'm not packing.

I don't go out on repo jobs armed, too much potential for trouble, especially if a passing cop mistakes me for a car thief. If one of Paradise Valley's finest hassles me while I'm picking up a bounty I just flash my official *Bail Bond Recovery Agent* badge and they leave me to it. They don't question the legality of my barely concealed piece. When I'm on a repossession gig I don't have a badge, just a bit of paperwork. It only takes a few seconds to flash the paperwork, but if a curious cop sees my gun I get to stand against the nearest handy wall with my legs spread for the next half-hour or so.

It's a pain in the ass.

I hardly ever need to defend myself anyway. Mostly I'm sneaky enough to never get caught, but when I do my appearance is usually enough to keep me out of a fight. As I've said before both *Big* and *Ugly* have their advantages, but mostly it's my red skin. Strange but true, most white people still believe in their hearts that the next great Indian uprising is just around the corner, and that instead of arrows and spears we'll use casino money to arm ourselves with Kalashnikovs and shoulder-fired rockets.

And on the occasions when *Big, Ugly* and *Red* aren't enough, I can defend myself. Some people seem to enjoy the challenge and the real scrappers usually turn out to be the ones you least suspect.

I'm not at all averse to laying out the occasional unruly drunk or mouthy asshole, it's actually very therapeutic, but only recreationally. I like my work to go smoothly. Also, Uncle Higheagle doesn't like me lumping up his customers unless I absolutely have to, even the ones who sometimes forget to make their payments for three or four consecutive months.

The sound of feet scraping blacktop behind me stopped and after a few more steps I stopped too, pulling the mostly empty pack of Camels from my breast pocket and lighting up. I turned as I cupped my hands against a light breeze and found my drunken shadow leaning deep into the thrift store's donation bin.

I stood my ground, smoking my Camel down to the butt, and when he still hadn't moved I approached him. Ten feet away, my suspicion hardened to a near certainty, and at five his rough snoring confirmed what I thought. I passed the sleeping man on my way back to Finke's, and heard the rattle of his garage door ascending once again.

Keeping close to the side of the building, I edged to the corner, and saw the Mustang pulling back out into the alley. There was no showboating this time. The lights were off. Something I couldn't identify occupied the front passenger seat next to Finke. The bodybuilder and tattoo guy filled the rear seat.

I could hear the sound of their conversation over the Mustang's idling growl, but couldn't make out the words.

Even as I tried to prepare myself for the disappointment of a wasted night, Finke opened the driver door and slid out. The other two followed, and Finke rounded on them. A few more seconds of indecipherable conversation followed, and Finke continued to the back door of his house, the body builder a few steps behind.

Mr. Tattoo remained behind with the Mustang.

There it was, my only chance to salvage my night's work. If I let Finke get back to his ride they would be gone, and I didn't have a chance in hell of keeping up on foot, long legs or not. To do it though, I'd have to get past, or go through, the tattoo guy.

I cogitated, and the tattoo guy walked around the back of the Mustang, giving Finke's rear door a quick glance.

Not quite ready to give up the building's shadows, I stood, waiting to move one way or the other.

Tattoo moved a few steps closer to the shop's open bay door, and after a moment of indecision, he left his post and went inside. I'm not above taking a lucky break when one is presented.

Moving quickly from my shadow and into the brightness of the parking lot's security lights, though not quite running, I closed the fifty yards to the Mustang.

Curiosity demanded I have a look inside Finke's shop to see what distraction had made my night's work much easier than it should have been, but I didn't waste any time. I eased myself into the idling Mustang's driver seat, put her in gear, and left the tattoo guy behind, still bent over the line he was snorting from the polished surface of the mini-bar.

I exited the alley onto Second Street, shifting up for my getaway, I heard shouts of alarm and anger from behind. I heard something else too, something I at first thought was the smoky, cracked laughter of Finke's unhappy neighbor, Rita. Before I hit third gear, blowing clean through the stop sign at the intersection and speeding toward the port district, I realized that the sound was not laughter, but agitation, and unless Finke and his associates had somehow shrunk Rita to the size of, say, a largish bird, it was not his neighbor making the fuss.

I pulled the shroud from the cage in the passenger seat, and met Trouble.

I'd never seen the bird before so I didn't know if its name actually was Trouble.

"Awk! Trouble! Here comes trouble!"

I used my powers of deductive reasoning, an ability my Uncle often calls into doubt, and deduced. I assumed.

As a rule, one should never trust my assumptions, but as the subject of my assumption seemed of small importance at the moment I didn't bother to second guess myself.

"Beer me, bitch!" Trouble advised.

"Shut up!"

"Blow me!"

The bird seemed uninterested in reasonable discourse,

so I abandoned my attempts to reason with it and concentrated on driving.

Trouble was not so easily dissuaded and continued its verbal abuse as I put blocks between us and Finke's place. I watched for pursuit and saw none. If either of Finke's pals had their own rides, they had not been quick enough to catch my trail. Not completely satisfied with that second assumption, one of much greater importance, I thought, I continued past the gunsmith's shop, past the block of scuzzy cabins that only the poor or shameless could call home, and turned right at the next intersection.

Trouble continued to squawk and bitch and I continued driving for another fifteen minutes, turning and doubling back at random, before I felt safe to go home.

"Pop the trunk, Musclehead," Trouble squawked as I pulled into the spot next to my cabin, the one usually reserved for my beat-to-shit Ventura.

I thought I'd managed to outrun trouble that night, the kind that likes to sneak up behind you and bite you on the ass before busting your beak as opposed to the kind that merely insults you while flapping around its cage.

The thing with trouble is that sometimes it comes along uninvited for the ride.

———

What I knew about caring for birds you could fit up a bug's ass and still have room for a cork, but I heard somewhere that if you stick their head beneath their wing or throw a blanket over their cage, they go to sleep. I didn't feel like sticking my hands anywhere near Trouble's head, or its meathook of a beak, so I draped the shroud back over the cage and waited.

The bird did not go to sleep, but the cloth muffled its squawks and insults enough that I wasn't worried about waking the neighbors.

I'd take the bird, along with whatever personal shit Finke kept in the Mustang, to Uncle Higheagle the next day, but it looked like I was stuck with the noisy, feathered turd for the rest of the night.

I jogged to the front door, the cage hanging from my left hand, while I exchanged the Mustang's keys for the ring in my pocket.

The bird's barrage of insulting chatter subsided to agitated whistles and hoots.

I let myself inside, setting my unexpected company on the floor beside the closet and opened the door. On the floor beside a clutter of boots and an old toolbox was a rolled up canvas car cover.

I grabbed the car cover and went back to the Mustang, closing the front door against Trouble's ill-natured babble. I heard the bird shout again through the door, singing some kind of jingle. I wasn't paying that close of attention. I was in a hurry to shroud the Mustang before Finke and his chums could get lucky and bumble down my street.

I was ready for the night to be over. Cover the Mustang and get back inside and try for a few hours of dreamless sleep.

Pop the trunk, Musclehead!

An odd thing for a bird to say, an odd thing for any animal to say for that matter.

I pulled the cover across the front of the car and

unraveled it over the windshield and open cab. I was about to let the shroud's tail fall over the back bumper when my curiosity got the better of me.

I fished the keys from my pocket, shuffled through the half-dozen or so hanging from Finke's pot-leaf fob until I had the right one, then opened the trunk.

The girl was young. Eighteen, maybe, but only by the skin of her teeth. Sixteen or seventeen wasn't out of the question, it was hard to be sure the way teenage girls dressed these days.

She was a good-looking girl, or would have been but for the blue-gray hue to her skin and the explosive smell of shit around her. She was half curled into a fetal position, eyes open and glassy, her one visible arm puckered with needle marks, old and fresh.

Dead.

She appeared to have been hastily dressed, post mortem, her tight little denim shorts pulled up but not buttoned, a dark, cherry-shaped birthmark just below her navel exposed. Her tank top shirt pulled on crooked and inside out. There was a small pink purse next to her, thrown in casually at her feet, its contents spilled around them.

I reached for the matching pink billfold poking demurely from the open purse, suppressing the urge to just slam the trunk and run back into my place. I forced myself to reach all the way in and pick up the billfold, knowing damn well that the girl's corpse was not about to sit upright and grab me, unable to transfer that knowing from my head to my gut. When I stepped back again, the girl's billfold in hand, I was able to breathe again.

I opened it and the first thing I saw was her driver's license displayed behind a cloudy and cracked plastic cover. I slid it free and saw the face, a little fresher, a lot less dead, of the woman in the trunk. I had to bend down closer to the trunk's light to read her name.

Candice Reynolds, eighteen. I had no doubt the men she partied with, Finke and his posse among them, would call her Candy while they shot her up and did things to her, telling her in evocative tones how much they'd just love to eat her up.

It's probably what I'd say.

I slid Candy's license back inside its holder, riffled through picture pockets. I found one of Candy looking slightly younger and much more innocent. The backdrop was vaguely familiar, rising green hills with narrow, paved lanes wandering across them like stone capillaries. Then I saw the sand trap and knew the place; Quail Ridge Country Club, set smack in the middle of a well-to-do neighborhood known casually as Snob Knob.

Candice Reynolds was a rich girl gone wild.

I slid the photo out, dropped her billfold back onto the purse, flipped the photo over to see if Candy had thought to note the specifics of the special occasion forever recorded on Kodak glossy; the date, the event, the home address of her next of kin. Anything.

There was writing, old and a bit smudged, but I didn't get the chance to read it.

"Hey, dickhead."

I slipped the picture into my t-shirt's breast pocket as I turned. I never got a chance to finish that turn either. I saw Musclehead's fist in my periphery for just a moment before it connected with my temple.

It was like being punched by an eighteen-wheeler.

First I saw stars zipping through the gray jelly of my brain like fireworks.

Then I saw nothing for a while.

If you're still hanging with me then I will assume that you're either interested in my story or you're a sadist and just enjoy watching me get knocked around. Either way, this should please. As to why I'm sticking it here, just when things were getting exciting ... well, maybe I'm a bit of a sadist too.

Don't worry, this is a short trip down memory lane, and it was the memory my battered brain puked up after I caught Musclehead's sucker-punch with my head.

It was sunny and stone cold outside, the grass sparkling with frost, Grandma Higheagle sparkling with costume jewelry, my favorite uncle there at her side. He was uncharacteristically solemn. I stood apart from them; a boy too tall for his age, skinny, marked by my recent beating and scarred by beatings past, looking like an accidental mourner in my street clothes. Just some boy who'd come along uninvited and refused to leave. No mother or father at my side. My only sib, a sister four years older than me, was gone by then, no one knew where. My father's sole contribution to my life, ignoring the raw genetics he'd provided, a face not even a mother could love, was to name me. I'm not sure which I resented more, the face or the name.

Your father was worthless as a cock-flavored sucker but he had a wicked good sense of humor.

The name he'd stuck me with before skipping town, presumably with a smile on his face and a beer in his hand, was Hieronymus.

Hieronymus Quick.

Yeah, the man was a fucking laugh-riot.

Like big sis, I never found out where he ended up. Not that I ever really looked.

So it was just mom, and I, and she was the focus of the morning's ritual.

Her funeral.

She'd died four days earlier, and it was a long time before I found out how. All I knew then is that she left one night like she did most every night, her feet unsteady and her head somewhere near the moon, hysterical and laughing and enraged all at the same time. Only that time she never came home. A few days later a man showed up, said she owed him money. When she wasn't there to pay, he quite naturally expressed his displeasure to me.

Neighbors heard, the tribal police came, and a few hours later I was identifying the body of a Jane Doe discovered the night before by a long haul driver who had stopped to take a piss on the side of the road. Their Jane Doe turned out to be Janice Quick, formerly Janice Higheagle. The police dropped me off with my grandma, my mom's mom, and she sent me walking back home as soon as their taillights faded from view. I didn't see her or any of my family on the reservation until the funeral, and even there they wouldn't look at me, standing there on my own in a torn and dirty t-shirt and pants too short for me.

I didn't understand why then, but I think I do now. I think they were afraid to acknowledge my healing cuts and cigarette burns, the fading bruises, and maybe afraid of what they might see in my eyes if I looked back.

Then one head did turn, and my Uncle Joey Higheagle regarded me with some confusion. He hadn't been to the reservation in months, didn't know how bad things were at home. Then he left his mother's side and joined me. He never said a word, just stood beside me.

He's stood with me since.

It was my uncle who called me Butch— *I'd have named you Butch . . . you look like a Butch to me*—and I decided to keep it.

That was the second best day of my life, the day I left my mother behind and went to live with Uncle Higheagle.

And like a memory within a memory I heard my mother's voice.

Boy, you may not be good for much, but you got ugly down to a science.

I remembered that gem as they lowered her into the ground, and before I could stop myself, I smiled. It must not have been a very loving one, because that was when Grandma Higheagle finally decided to grace me with her notice. Her expression was positively evil.

I was young and full of rage and hurt, I didn't give a

damn what she thought of me anymore. I stopped giving a damn about a lot of things, and it felt good to not care anymore.

Don't worry, not all of my stories are downers. Some of them are actually pretty funny.

CHAPTER 6

I awoke from a dream of free falling and felt myself bounce around inside a moving box with a steel lid. My landing was abrupt and soft, a plushly carpeted steel box then. The trunk of a car, and a big one if someone had managed to stuff me into it. A Cadillac, maybe, or a Crown Vic. Another bump bounced me, and something beside me tipped over and bounced against my head.

Something that felt like ribbed steel. A birdcage.

Trouble squawked his irritation a moment later, confirming my suspicions.

"Here comes trouble!" He screeched, told me to fuck myself.

Laughter from the cab.

I suppose it was pretty funny.

I tried to keep track of the minutes as they, whoever they might be, sped me away. Trying to figure out where they might be taking me by estimating the miles. After two minutes I realized I had no idea how long I'd been snoozing, or which of the roads out of town I was on, and gave up.

Another bump, another roll around the carpeted steel box. Trouble squawked again. It was starting to get old.

I reached for my cell phone but it was gone. My hands were bound in front of me with something that felt like an industrial strength zip tie. The car slowed for a sharp corner, there was the familiar rumble of train tracks beneath me, and I threw my weight forward, using inertia to roll myself into a hunched sitting position. It was cramped, my head was a bit closer to my ass than I usually like it, but it was better than the loose, head-thumping tumbles I'd been enjoying.

I was pretty sure I knew where they were taking me now. The sharp twist of the road, the rumble of train tracks, and the sharp, broccoli-fart smell of the cannery that runs from July to September every summer. Or maybe it was just that my nose was nestled somewhat uncomfortably between my ass-cheeks.

Unless is *was* my own ass I was smelling, we were on Washington State Road 193, the Wawawai Road, which follows the Snake River east for about twenty miles before twisting up the mountains into the high plains and shit-kicker country.

The car sped up again and I rocked forward, thumping the nape of my neck against the trunk latch. Trouble's cage rolled with me, striking the back of the trunk with a rattle.

"Motherfucker," I groaned, reaching up with my bound hands to rub my throbbing head.

"Motherfucker," Trouble agreed, then whistled. It was

a happy sound. "Motherfucker motherfucker motherfucker!" Another happy whistle.

I wondered idly if I'd managed to teach him a new word.

More laughter from the cab. Two distinct voices.

Mr. Muscles and the walking tattoo.

Finke would be driving the Mustang, carrying his own freight of dead flesh.

I thought it was very likely Candy and I were about to meet again very soon, probably at the bottom of the river.

The most convenient place I could imagine for the reunion was Granite Rock, a high, climbing slab of solid granite jutting out over the slow water. Granite Rock was remote, Granite Rock was big, and the slow moving water beneath its jutting lip was deep.

Granite Rock had been a popular party spot for a lot of years. The occasional drunken gang rape and drowning did nothing to discourage the local teens who used the spot. It was the Satanists who finally scared them off. Stray cats and dogs hung disemboweled from inverted crosses, pentagrams painted in their blood, weird runes and pictographs that had nothing to do with Satan, or even with Christianity, those were the things that finally killed the decades-long party that sometimes took a few days off, but never stopped completely.

If I had a couple of bodies I wanted to dump discreetly in the night, I couldn't think of a better place than Granite Rock to do it.

"I'm bringing sexy back," Trouble confided to me.

I found myself hoping Mr. Muscles and the walking tattoo would do the right thing and kill the bird too.

I should make it clear that I did not intend to just let them kill me. If they wanted me dead they were going to have to work for it. I tested the strength of the plastic zip tie binding my wrists, even while I deduced our destination and tried to estimate the time left until we arrived. I gave myself another five minutes, ten if I was very lucky. I had an idea they didn't have to do this sort of thing very often, otherwise they would have bound my hands behind my back. Right or wrong, the idea was a small comfort, like a dim light in a locked but spacious trunk.

A light would have been nice. Even a dim one.

I felt for the latch I'd thumped my neck against and found it after a minute or so of fumbling. It might have been the only piece of bare metal in the well carpeted box. It wasn't sharp, but if I could work the tie into the groove where the latch tongue caught, I might make it work.

I had to bend my wrists painfully, pressing the palms of my hands flat against the back of the carpeted trunk. The zip tie finally slipped into the metal groove and I began to work it back and forth, up and down, my hands slipping around over the carpet's rough fibers. It felt like feeling up the world's most hairy-chested woman.

"Shit or get off the pot," Trouble advised.

It was sound advice. My semi-erotic exploration of the trunk's rear was getting me nowhere. The metal was too smooth. It wouldn't cut through the plastic of the zip tie.

Clenching my teeth in grim anticipation, a down payment on the pain to come, I pressed the zip tie harder into the groove. My wrists screamed in hyperextended indignation, and the thin plastic of the zip tie bit into my skin.

The car began to turn, to slow.

We had arrived.

I yanked down, doubling over until my nose actually did touch my ass, putting as much weight into the motion as I could. The palms of my hands dragged hard, flaring in pain from the carpet burn. I felt skin and hair tear away from my wrists as the zip tie bit in.

Then it snapped, and my hands were free.

We slowed again, then with a gravel-crunching slide, we stopped.

The momentum rolled me onto my back, my head thumping the floor again with a muffled bang. Enjoying their newfound freedom, my hands ventured out to either side, my fingers curling into the carpet. I braced myself and curled as tight as my inconveniently lanky frame allowed, bringing my knees to my chin and putting my boots flat against the lid of the trunk.

I held my breath, waited.

Even Trouble was silent; not a mutter or squawk. Not even the rustle of his wings against his cage's bars.

Doors slammed, one, then a second, and I heard footsteps kicking up gravel from the rest area parking lot. The footsteps stopped at my end of the car, and for a second I thought I could hear the jingle of keys.

I gave up my grip on the trunk's carpet and laced my fingers over my knees, pulling them in a bit closer.

My feet hovered just below the lid of the trunk.

There was a scrape of the key turning inside the lock, a click as the latch opened, and a creak as the lid began to lift.

I tensed, and let go of my knees, kicking straight up at the trunk lid with all my bunched strength. It made a satisfying double thump as it connected with both their heads. A better shot I could not have hoped for.

I saw them for just a moment, the scant starlight shining through the gap of the open trunk seemed bright after my short time in the perfect darkness. The trunk lid's momentum actually lifted the shorter Tattoo Guy from his feet. Then they were gone.

I heard the sound of two bodies hitting the dirt, two solid, inert thuds. If you dropped a couple two-hundred pound bags of shit from a high window, I'm pretty sure they'd make the same sound.

Trouble exploded into chattering motion inside his cage, his rapid-fire squawks sounding a lot like laughter.

I couldn t help myself. I started laughing with him.

It took almost a minute to unfold my body and pull myself out of the trunk, and by the time I managed it, the surety that Finke himself would be waiting just out of sight to clobber me again, or put a bullet in my head, had driven my inappropriately timed good humor underground.

The promise of death, or even just a solid head thumping, can be a real buzzkill.

Finke was not waiting for me. His two goons lay in the trash littered gravel, the muscle-bound guy blowing blood bubbles from his broken nose and mashed lips as he snored, the little tattoo covered guy not doing much of anything. His face was a mess, his nose clearly also broken, his dislocated jaw jutting pugnaciously past the bent tip of his schnoz. He looked like a man trying to eat his own face. What he wasn't doing was breathing. I wasn't positive but I thought open and blank eyes were a good indication.

Since it wasn't exactly an ice-cream social he'd brought me on, I didn't let it bum me out too much.

Musclehead was unarmed, there were no guns on or around him. He wore a *Gold's Gym* tank top, it looked painted on, and a pair of Bermuda shorts that looked ready to bust open at the seams. I could only think of one place where he might have a gun concealed, and I wasn't going to check there no matter how desperate the situation. There was a gun lying next to Tattoo's outstretched hand.

I picked Tattoo's gun up, checked the magazine and then made it safe before tucking it in the waistband of my pants. Shooting my joy-stick off in a moment of carelessness would take much of the pleasure out of my narrow escape.

Finally, feeling firmly in charge of the situation, for the time being anyway, I decided to satisfy my curiosity regarding the two assholes on the ground.

Tattoo's wallet was a scarred and filthy leather billfold anchored to his belt by a chain. Tucked inside it was a surprising amount of cash, all in fifties and one-hundreds, a half-dozen credit cards, all issued to different people, and a license with his narrow, acne-scarred mug on it. I left the cash and cards, but took his license and slipped it into my pocket with the picture of Candy.

Musclehead's wallet was harder to extract, trapped at the bottom of a deep rear pocket and buried under his freight of muscles. I had to roll him over onto his stomach and dig so deep that anyone passing the scene at that moment might have thought we were engaged in some rough petting. Again there was a respectable amount of cash, all large bills, but no credit cards or driver's license. The only thing with a name on it was his Gold's Gym membership card, so I added that to my stash.

As I rose, Musclehead began to groan, then to stir. I had a decision to make; let him wake up and make him talk. Maybe take him with me and let him explain the situation to the cops. If it had been anyone else I might have gone that way, but I didn't like my chances against him if he decided to make trouble for me. I'm a big boy, maybe six inches taller than Musclehead, but he'd already proven he could one-punch me, and the thought of those meathooks he called hands maybe closing around my throat was a bad one. He wouldn't even have to choke me to death, he could just crush my throat or snap my neck like a toothpick.

I pulled Tattoo's gun, and considered it for a moment. It was a Hi-Point 9mm, the scumbag's weapon of choice, Posey might have called it. Prone to jams, inaccurate, and a pain in the ass to maintain, but dirt-cheap.

I didn't like the idea of this guy coming after me for a little payback but I couldn't quite bring myself to shoot him in cold blood. I gave him a good, solid thump on the back of his skull instead, once again easing a small pang of guilt by reminding myself that I was not in fact being chauffeured to a surprise party. Most likely my night's itinerary would have been a quick cap in the head and a trip to the bottom of the river.

Besides, I owed this guy a lump or two.

I gave Tattoo a last look, my suspicion that I'd killed the guy growing a little stronger, then turned to their ride.

A Lincoln Town Car, late '80s, which explained the ample trunk-space. Painted jet black, it almost blended into the night. Both front doors were open, the dome light illuminating a red interior that matched the custom pinstriping, leather seats and all.

It struck me as funny, like a joke so bad that you have to laugh at its absurdity. If not for the tattoo's corpse laying a few feet behind me, I *might* have laughed.

Not exactly a mob car, a real mob car would have been a bit less conspicuous, but certainly the car of someone who liked to pretend they were a mobster. A faux wise guy. A Sopranos wannabe.

I found the keys hanging from the trunk's lock and pulled them free. I was about to slam it closed when my little blue friend piped up again. I'd forgotten all about him in my excitement over not being dead.

A few minutes earlier I would have been happy to see the thing plucked and roasting on a spit, but in light of my own good fortune I decided to extend the hand of amnesty and rescue the little shit. I figured the death option would still be open further down the road if I changed my mind, but I was sufficiently freaked out at the moment that I felt better pushing forward with a bit of company.

He would be easy company at least. I wouldn't have to hold up my end of the conversation.

I dropped Trouble's cage onto the front passenger seat, belted him in, slammed the door.

Bright lights stabbed at me from the winding road

back to the city. Behind them, the sharp and glossy red body of my favorite Mustang came into view and veered across the center lane toward the Granite Rock parking area.

It was time to get the fuck outta there.

Before I could take my first step around the front of the Lincoln to the driver's side, a large fist got up-close and personal with the back of my aching skull.

CHAPTER 7

I fell forward against the Lincoln's passenger door, then stumbled sideways when I tried to push myself upright again. My head throbbed like a bass drum. There was a whisper of wind against my left ear as something passed within an inch of it and a crunch, the sound of a fleshy impact against metal. The big car rocked with the impact.

"Fuck," from behind me; Musclehead's reasonable reaction to punching a Lincoln Town Car.

"Fuck!" Trouble squawked in fervent agreement.

My bell was still ringing too loudly to log an opinion, but my equilibrium was coming back. I pushed myself back from the car, managed to stay on my feet, spun to face the big turd who kept hitting me.

There were two of them, but only for a few seconds. I shook my head, blinked, and the two fuzzy muscle-bound men resolved themselves into one.

He hopped in place, bent over and cradling his fist, then looked up at me, bared his teeth, charged.

He actually roared, like a bull. It was pretty funny.

I think he meant to tackle me.

I met his charge with a smile and a fist.

A second later I was the one screaming and cradling my fist. That fucker had a hard skull.

He stumbled back, still bent double, his arms pinwheeling for balance. Behind him the ground dropped away sharply toward the river. Never one to pass up a lucky break when one comes along, I helped him on his way. I closed the distance between us in five long strides, doing my own bull impression. He was still stumbling in a daze when I collided with him. Even dazed and off balance it was like hitting a brick wall, but I was a slightly larger brick wall, so it was Musclehead that staggered backward. I watched him stumble over the edge and disappear as I stumbled and fell to my knees in the dust and gravel, tearing the hell out of a new pair of pants and skinning a pair of slightly used knees.

My knee-bound shadow leapt forward as a set of bright lights hit me from behind, and the sound of tires sliding through gravel gave me just enough warning to roll out of the way when something a little bigger and made of steel tried to do the same.

I saw the man piloting the Mustang rise, saw something unpleasant in his raised hand, and scurried for cover behind the back of the Lincoln.

Two shots followed me, kicking up dust and gravel behind my feet, and a third ricocheted off the corner of the Lincoln's rear bumper a second after I dove behind it. I landed on the tattoo man, who was slightly softer than the ground, but also dead, which was gross.

I rolled away, and shouted in unexpected agony as

something hard and made of metal jabbed me sharply in the groin.

The dead man's gun, still tucked deep in my waist-band. I'd forgotten all about it.

I blamed my recent knocks on the noggin. Hit a guy in the head too many times and something is bound to shake loose and fall out. I was slightly impressed that I remembered to flip the safety off before rising and giving Finke a little back. I fired blindly as soon as I'd cleared the Lincoln's trunk. Three shots as rapidly as my trigger finger allowed.

The first shot blew out the Mustang's front passenger side tire. The second punched a large and ugly hole through the driver's side door, shredding the upholstery, tearing metal, shattering the rolled down window. The third passed uselessly through the air where Finke was standing only a second earlier.

Shattered glass tinkled down inside the ruined driver's door. The deflating tire blew me a raspberry.

Uncle Higheagle wasn't going to thank me for that.

I spotted Finke a second later rushing around the front of the Mustang, his gun leading the way, and ducked low. I shuffled behind the cab, hoping the tinted windows would hide me, and waited for the gunfire to resume. It didn't.

No gunfire, no rough purr of the Mustang's engine, no footsteps crunching in the gravel. Even the fucking bird was quiet. The new silence was as sharp as a razor. I could almost feel it cutting the night. I hated it.

Wherever Finke was now, he was laying low. Waiting.

"Hey, Finke!"

A short pause, then Finke responded. "Yo!"

I couldn't get a lock on him, his voice echoed in the narrow river valley, seemed to come from everywhere at once. I only knew that he was still somewhere on the other side of the big black Lincoln. He sounded . . . amused.

"Feel like talking this over?"

"Talk it over? You fucking kidding me?" He laughed, but there was no humor in it. "You tried to steal my fuckin' car!"

While he spoke I slowly lowered myself to the ground and peered beneath the Lincoln. I wondered if it would help to tell him I was just a repo man, decided it probably wouldn't.

I searched for a pair of feet in the diffuse glow of the Mustang's headlights, but they were pointed the wrong way and there were just too many fucking shadows. I couldn't find Finke's feet, but I did spot the Lincoln's keys in the gravel beneath the passenger door.

Shit.

"You still with us?" Finke, sounding amused again. It was still impossible to place him. He knew where I was though. I could imagine him smiling, and imagined myself putting a fist through that smile.

I rose to a crouch again. Time to relocate.

"Yep," I waddled back a few steps, toward the front of the big car. Gravel ground underfoot, but if I couldn't hear him move, maybe he couldn't hear me. Time to shut my mouth and see if I could get around on his blind side, or what I hoped was his blindside.

"*Why* did you steal my car?"

I turned on the move, ducked a little lower but knew I

couldn't stay hidden once I passed the cab. My head would be a solitary duck in a midnight shooting gallery.

"*Boss!*"

What? I hadn't expected to hear that voice anytime soon.

"What?" Finke sounded as surprised as I felt. He stood up, forgetting our cat and mouse game in his surprise. He'd been crouched low behind the hood, his feet hidden behind the tire. His gun was still pointed at the point where my head would have been if I'd taken one more step, but he faced the river.

I grinned and stood, stepping out from behind the cab for a better shot. Beyond us, spotlighted by the Mustang's dimming headlights, Musclehead pulling himself up over the edge. Our eyes met.

"Behind you!" He tried to point and lost his grip. He slid back out of sight.

Finke jumped like a cat in a frying pan and spun to face me.

I had a bead on him, right between his eyes, and pulled the trigger before he could get me in his sights.

Click.

Empty.

Shit.

He stood for a second with his mouth open in an expression of dumb shock. Gotta admit, it suited him. Before he could wise up to the fact that he was still breathing I used the gun again in the only way I could. I threw it, and from a distance of only three or four feet the impact was most satisfying. It whacked him butt first in the center of his forehead and bounced into the darkness, leaving a nice red welt. His eyes crossed and turned up, as if trying to inspect the damage, and he staggered backward a few steps.

I ran around the front of the car to finish him, but he'd retained enough of his senses for a retreat back toward the Mustang. He dove for cover behind it, and for a second I considered following him. But he still had a working gun, and I could hear Musclehead struggling his way back up the cliff toward us.

An old, dark friend whispered in my ear— *fuck it! Go get him!* —and I almost did. I wanted to tap-dance on his gonads and bounce on his chest and force-feed him my fist, but obeying that jolly and suicidally insane voice usually only made things worse. Sometimes I think it wanted me to die.

And if I stood there any longer to consider my options, it would get its wish.

I bent and scooped the Lincoln's keys from the gravel as Musclehead resurfaced and Finke began to shout at me, his complacent, just passing the time until I shoot you voice, was gone. He sounded like a toddler having a tantrum.

The part of me that wanted to pull Finke and his scumbags apart like Barbie dolls and see how they looked with all their parts mixed and matched settled into sulking silence in its dark cave at the back of my cranium.

Roughly ten minutes after arriving at Granite Rock, trussed and trunked and ready for cement boots, I pulled back onto the road back to town, throwing rooster tails of gravel and dirt over the corpse of the walking tattoo. I had only the vaguest idea of the trouble I was headed back into and no idea how many more of Finke's fuck-sticks were waiting for me back in West Paradise Valley, but I knew where I might find one of them.

It would take me too close for comfort to Finke's place, but I didn't have a lot of options.

I had a few stops to make along the way too.

It was going to be a long night.

CHAPTER 8

I didn't expect a clean escape. Wawawai Road was a bottleneck, a twisting and narrow two-lane with no exits until the Wawawai Bicentennial Bridge, more popularly known these days as Redwolf Bridge, the way back into the city. I pushed the big car beyond its safe speed, but if Finke got the Mustang going he'd still be on my ass like stink on a hippie. It would only take a few minutes to drop Candy into the drink, a few more to slap on the spare tire she'd been keeping company in the trunk. He wouldn't even need to bother with a jack now that Musclehead was back with the program. I suspected he'd already called his friends for help and that I'd find the road blocked ahead. My guts tightened as I put miles between myself and Granite Rock, my suspicion growing to a certainty. Then I hit the final short, straight stretch before the bridge across the Snake River, and then the bridge itself came into view, a big concrete arch that I was way too familiar with.

The city was in sight and I had a clear road.

I began to relax.

If you've followed me up to this point you probably know what comes next, at least in general terms. I however didn't see it coming.

It's what I get for relaxing.

Lights exploded the darkness behind me; red, blue, white, flashing. Blinding me through my rearview mirror.

A cop car left its hiding spot behind a billboard for the Tribal Casino and tore after me. I wasn't speeding, wasn't swerving from lane to lane, but I didn't waste time wondering why the cops were giving me the *pull over*. Considering the circumstances I was thrilled to see someone in a uniform take an interest. Someone who actually got paid for this kind of shit was about to take over for me. I decided I could deal with that.

Despite what Uncle Higheagle thinks, I do not get off on this kind of shit. I would rather have been at home sleeping.

There was a wide gravel turnout across from Redwolf Bridge, a wide spot for trucks turning onto the bridge. I pulled into it, hurriedly slipping the seatbelt on before I killed the ignition. Happy as I was to see the men in blue, I didn't want to tempt a ticket for not using my seatbelt. They take that shit seriously in Washington.

I rolled down my window and waited.

My first sign that this wasn't a routine stop was the drawn gun, a Beretta .45 ACP, as the officer approached the Lincoln. My second sign was when he stuck it in my face and ordered me to hand over the keys.

My brain has never been good at speed shifting. For a moment I was only able to stare down the barrel of the gun leveled at my face.

"Hand over the keys, sir!" The officer's empty left hand extended, open palm up, into the cab. He snapped his fingers for emphasis.

It's times like this that I kick myself for not having a cache of clever responses. An action hero is supposed to have good lines for such occasions.

I settled for my standard bewildered look as I moved to comply.

"Slowly," he barked with the authority which only a blue uniform can lend. "Nice and easy does it."

Always eager to please, I moved with exaggerated slowness, reaching for the keys dangling from the ignition then pulling them free.

He snapped the fingers of his left hand again, a sound almost as jagging to my nerves as, say, a monkey raping a cat.

I was extending the keys toward that open hand when another light joined the circus. No red and blue this time, only headlights. I watched their approach in my side mirror as the good officer turned toward them, and the police cruiser's strobing dome lights threw the grill of the slowing car into colorful relief. It was a grill I recognized immediately, belonging to one of my favorite classics.

It was a '68 Mustang.

It pulled in behind the parked police cruiser. Blue light washed over the shaven dome of Musclehead's melon, making it look like corpse-flesh.

"I got your man here, Cameron," the cop said, withdrawing his free hand from my open window to shield his eyes from the Mustang's headlights. "You wanna turn your fucking lights off?"

The situation had officially gone from bad to worse.

Without stopping to consider what kind of new shit I was stepping in—probably a good thing, thinking was never my strong point—I pulled my hand with the keys back inside and reached for the cop's gun with my other hand. My hands are large and I was able to get a decent grip on his piece before he knew I was even reaching for it. Before he could tighten his own grip, I yanked it free of his hand.

In the old spaghetti westerns I used to love when I was a kid, the ones where I always rooted for the Indians instead of the cowboys even though I knew the Indians never won, gunshots are only slightly more intimidating than, say, the sound a bottle rocket makes when it pops thirty feet or so overhead. In real life the sound is much more startling, and when the gunshot happens to go off six inches from your ear in the cab of a car, words like loud, startling, or earsplitting don't even cover it.

The sound of the cop's gun discharging as I yanked it out of his hand, causing his curled index finger to tighten on the trigger, didn't so much startle me as nearly make me shit my pants. It wasn't earsplitting, it was skull-splitting.

The passenger window exploded in a rain of sparkling shards and chips, the police cruiser's flashing lights painting them in ruby, sapphire, and amethyst hues.

The cop shrieked in shock and anger, Finke shouted in surprise, and Musclehead, perhaps thinking their cop had just offed me, shouted with glee.

Trouble went into a rage inside his cage. He was a blue and gold tornado of feathers, squawks, and expletives.

Still holding the gun by its hot barrel, ignoring the way the burn of hot gunmetal and the white agony of the powder burn fanning down my arm from wrist to elbow, I swept the butt of the gun smartly across the cop's face.

He went to his knees with a satisfying grunt of pain. Before Finke or his goon could react I took advantage of my continuing dumb-shit luck and threw the Lincoln's door wide. The door finished what I started, smacking the kneeling cop full in the face and laying him out flat. As I jumped out I saw Musclehead ducking behind the Mustang's dashboard, reaching toward the glove box, and Finke tugging at his own piece tucked perhaps a little too snugly in his waistband. Before either could produce their guns I pulled the punch-drunk cop to his feet in front of me and shoved the gun in his back.

"Don't move," I said, trying to sound large and in charge, trying to sound convincing. Trying to sound like I hadn't just about shit my pants. I nodded toward the river sweeping lazily past only a stone's throw away. "Toss 'em now. I'll clock this guy out for the night."

Musclehead stopped, watched me warily, made no moves.

"Ah, fuck 'im," Finke said, and pulled his piece.

At those words my intuition, not to mention my dumb-ass luck, failed me.

"Hey . . . no!" The cop made a feeble effort to extract himself.

Finke shot him.

The bang of Finke's gun wasn't as apocalyptic as the gunshot in the cab of the old Town Car, but it was still plenty loud. For a moment, I really thought I was dead.

There was a whiff of something like burning doll hair, then the cop smacked into me like a wall of blue polyester.

Down I went, the bad cop landing on top of me with a cry of pain. I experienced the classic fade to black, a long, dark tunnel, and a feeling I was disconnected from my body. I hoped like hell there was a welcoming white light somewhere ahead.

It was the continued squawking from Trouble that convinced me I was still in the game. Good dogs may go to heaven, but I don't think a loving God would chose to reward heaven's residents with an eternity of Trouble's agitated squawks and profane directives.

"Go fuck yourself!" *Squawk!*

"Got 'im" Finke shouted.

"Got 'em both," Musclehead corrected, and chuckled.

But had they?

The darkness had receded, not death, but a mere moment of unconsciousness, and I was now very much aware of being anchored to my body. It was sore from its latest tumble to the gravel, and there was a dead cop lying on top of it.

I felt the warm tackiness of blood on my chest, but not the pain of a bullet's entry. I didn't have time to consider this mystery. I heard the crunch of boots in gravel. Finke and Musclehead were on the way, and once they figured out I was still breathing their first priority would be to make me stop doing it.

As it turned out, dumb-shit luck was with me again. The cop's service gun was still clenched in my hand. I raised it, pointing it blindly in the direction of the approaching footfalls, fired.

Shouts of surprise, the sounds of clumsy retreat.

I didn't bother to check the accuracy of my aim, just rolled the dead cop off me and bolted for the Lincoln's open driver side door. I couldn't help one last look at the dead cop as I slammed the door closed and fumbled around the seat for the dropped keys. His shirt had come untucked during his fall, and I saw the hem of his Kevlar vest sticking out beneath his shirt's crumpled tail. Finke's slug had penetrated the vest on its entrance, but not on its exit.

"Here comes trouble," the bird said almost conversationally, his fury spent. Blue and gold feathers covered the passenger seat like alien confetti.

I threw two more shots back at them as I sped off, the cop's Beretta making a much more impressive bang than Finke's, showering gravel over the cop car in a rooster tail. I heard a slug punching through metal, a second shattering glass, and cringed.

It was not a good night to be a Mustang.

There was no further pursuit as I turned across the bridge and fled toward West Paradise Valley.

Running from a pair of snakes and into a whole den of them.

They'd let me go for the moment, they had a mess to clean up on the other side of Redwolf Bridge, but they'd be back on my ass again, and soon. Finke and all his scumbag friends.

I exited right off the city end of the bridge, avoiding the main drag through town in favor of the less populated port district. I did not go home right away, if any of Finke's asshole friends were sleazing around my neighborhood they'd recognize the big Lincoln in a second. I turned down Fifteenth Street toward the log yards.

I considered the situation as I drove.

Tattoo's piece was a 9mm, and since he obviously worked for Finke, I thought it was safe to assume Finke provided his firepower. Another assumption from the man with the dyslexic intuition, but assumption was all I had to work with.

I could think of only one 9mm round powerful enough to penetrate a Kevlar vest, steel-cored submachine gun ammo, loaded to higher pressure than standard handgun shells, and probably manufactured in one of the former commie block states of Eastern Europe. This bit of trivial gun knowledge was second-hand, gleaned over the years from Posey. While I had no previous personal experience with these 9mm hot loads, I considered Posey's tutorials the next best thing. As I think I've hinted before, when it came to guns and ammo, Posey's knowledge was absolute.

The basics of the steel-core 9mm hot load—dirty, unreliable as the guns Finke and his thugs used to fire them, and illegal. Definitely not available at your local Walmart.

I made a right on Industrial Way, so close to the river again that I could smell it, a dirty smell, but one I liked. The smell of home. I couldn't see the river, tall stacks of logs flanked Industrial Way for several blocks with only the occasional break between them, but neither could anyone on the other side of the river see me.

"Candy's handy and sweet to eat." Trouble clicked its beak and continued in a huckstering tone, almost like a carnival barker's sales pitch, "and Honey's wet and sticky."

Finke's exotic ammunition suggested likely Eastern European connections, and two unappealing possibilities —drugs or human trafficking, maybe both. Drugs was my guess. Candy at the very least was no import, she was homegrown.

Quite a leap, I know, but unless I could somehow trick Finke into the standard movie-show villain monologue, I would just have to settle for half-assed guesswork. I didn't think that was likely, if Finke did manage to catch me again I expected nothing less than a quick bullet in the head. He wouldn't be in a chatting mood.

The log yard ended at Ninth Street with a dirt parking lot, a large open-air shop, and a complex of trailers belonging to Chapman Logging.

I slowed, scanning the street ahead and behind for other cars, then turned off the Lincoln's lights and pulled into Chapman's parking lot. I cruised past the offices, past a fenced equipment yard, turned into the log yard.

The car jounced and bucked over rough bull rock as I guided it between two log piles. When I was well out of view of the road I killed the motor and rested a second to consider my next move.

Trouble was growing restless again, squawking and muttering. "I'm a bad bird."

"Shhh," I said, more out of reflex than hope the bird would actually hush up. To my happy surprise, Trouble mimicked my hushing, though a bit more quietly, and did hush.

I sat, I considered, and I came up with nothing new. So far my only possible lead was passed out in the donation bin of the local Goodwill. Even if he was still there the risk of venturing that close to Finke's place was not appealing. I was going to try it though. Nothing ventured and all that shit.

I popped the glove box open and swept out an odd assortment of junk, some contraband and some mundane, onto the seat and floor. After a short search I found what I needed, a ballpoint pen and a folded sheet of paper. I left the glove box door open and composed my plan B by its scant light. Just in case I didn't make it through the night.

Cameron Finke killed Candice Reynolds and a police officer last night. He has probably dumped their bodies in the river off of Granite Rock. He is coming after me now. If you get this note, take it to the local FBI, not the police.

Even though I knew how bug-shit paranoid it sounded, I bit my lip and finished the note.

Finke had at least one Paradise Valley cop in his pocket. I don't know who you can trust at the local cop shop.

I finished my note off with the date and time, as close as I could estimate it, and after a second's consideration decided not to put my John Hancock beneath it. I didn't like the idea of signing my name to this, just in case it was Finke and his goons that found it.

I was flipping the sheet over to smooth out the creases

when I saw the print on the other side; a web address in the top left hand corner, a header belonging to some internet hookup website, and an item titled *Party Girls*.

> Sweet, sexy, exotic dancers
> for one-on-one or group entertainment.
> Call or email anytime.
> Honey Beloi & Candy Roche.

I tore off a corner of the sheet and scribbled down the 888 number and email, then grabbed Trouble's cage and stepped into a tense, menacing night. If Honey knew who her business partner had spent the evening with then she was in danger. Least I could do was warn her.

I shouldn't call her, I thought. *I've got enough trouble of my own without adding hers to it.*

Good advice I knew. I also knew I wouldn't take it.

Offer me a piece of good advice and I always run from it as fast and far as I can. I'm stupid like that.

CHAPTER 9

I left the reservation the day of my mother's funeral, moved to Paradise Valley, what I always thought of as *The City*, as if it were the only city in the world.

I wasn't the only Indian at Sacajawea Middle School, but you could have counted us on your hands and had enough fingers left over to play with yourself. It's funny, my school on the res' was named after a white guy who came to Nez Perce country a hundred years ago to preach at the red-skinned heathens, and my school in Paradise Valley was named after an Shoshone girl who spent a few years keeping white explorers from being killed by their own ignorance. Our football team was called The Savages, changed to The Braves a year or so after I left for the larger hormone factory called high school. Some folks thought The Savages too offensive to be allowed and made a lot of noise until the school board changed it. I thought it was a perfect description for what the school board referred to as *The Student Body*.

Most kids between the ages of twelve and fifteen *are*

savages. They would have gone to classes naked, shit in the wastepaper baskets, eaten their teachers, and gang raped the cheerleading squad if they hadn't been conditioned from infancy not to do stuff like that. Some kids simply aren't trainable though. You know the kind of kids I'm talking about. You went to school with them, avoided them in the hallways, forbade your daughters to date them when it was their turn to be fed feet first into the education system.

I wasn't one of those kids.

Most kids define themselves by the opinions of others, their craven craving for attention and approval pushing all other considerations so far into the background that little things like learning drop right off the radar.

I wasn't one of those either. I had a few friends, but no one I couldn't live without.

People are just social animals, dogs walking on two legs instead of four, and if you crowd a bunch of us together we start to behave like it. We form packs.

Each pack has an alpha, the leader, and a beta, the second in command. Below the beta are the gammas and deltas, the suck-ups and followers. The lowest rung of the pack ladder belongs to the omega, the poor bastard who always tails behind the main group and eats their shit. Then there's the nomad, who exists outside the pack. You've seen them, usually walking alone with their heads down, their books clutched to their chest, their ankles nipped to bloody shreds.

That last bit is a metaphor, by the way. I don't think they allow biting in public schools.

If you think my low opinion of people in general is

unjustified then you haven't been paying attention to them.

I was a nomad, but the small packs that formed in my school mostly left me alone. I was bigger and uglier than their alphas.

My middle and high school career was all about doing the work and getting the hell out as quickly as I could. Mostly I stayed out of trouble and earned good grades, better grades than my teachers thought I had a right to sometimes. The teachers at Sacajawea were no more enlightened than your garbage man or the guy who flips your burgers at Mickey-Ds. They took one look at me and adjusted their opinions downward.

I could have drifted through middle and high school without a single incident, but I was stupid. I didn't like bullies, and bullies in packs really pissed me off.

Don't be tempted to think of my hatred of bullies as a noble thing, it wasn't. I wasn't interested being a hero, I didn't give a shit about helping the downtrodden. For me it was all about kicking the shit out of a pack of mean dogs and watching them crawl away.

Like I said, stupid.

It was the fall of my eighth grade year. September, football season, and I was on the football team's shit list.

Yeah, the entire team.

The coach had been trying to recruit me since I arrived at Sacajawea, and when he couldn't convince me he nagged Uncle Higheagle to make me join. My uncle was a booster, it was good for his various businesses to be active in community stuff, but he told the coach that his activism didn't extend to providing talent. When the coach pressed him, Uncle Higheagle invited him to have anal intercourse with himself.

Uncle Higheagle is very cool that way.

Then the harassment began. The team took their coach's grudge and ran with it.

By mid-September it was mostly finished, two of The Savages starting offensive linemen were now viewing the field through black eyes and *hut-hut-huting* through broken teeth. Defending yourself and inviting trouble are two different things though, so I avoided the football field during after-school practices. It was only a slight detour from my regular route home, but it was enough to get me in real trouble.

As usual, trouble came in the form of a girl.

Her name was Elizabeth Trout, and we shared classes at Sacajawea. Thanks to my trouble with *The Sacajawea Savages* we also shared a two-block stretch of street on our walks home from school. She was pretty, short black hair that made her white skin look even paler, just developing the good bits that made boys notice her. Not shy or overly social. She had friends but not a clique.

She was like me, an animal without a pack.

We noticed each other but never spoke. I was as happy to ignore her as she was to ignore me. Just two nomads who crossed paths but didn't feel obliged to sniff each other's ass-cracks.

One day as September blurred into October and Halloween decorations began to appear in the yards of the upper-middle-class East Paradise Valley homes, Elizabeth Trout ran across one of the meanest packs to form during my time at Sacajawea. They may have been waiting for her, but I think it was probably just her bad luck that day.

My bad luck too.

I was half a block from the corner where we always parted ways when I heard her first shout. Alarm, nothing more. She might have been startled by a dog or a car. Nothing for me to worry about, so I kept walking. Her second shout was anger. I ignored that too. Her third came before I was safely out of earshot, and that one I couldn't ignore.

It was a shriek of pain.

So I turned to see what was up. What happened next was unavoidable. Sometimes I just can't help myself.

There were five of them, three from our grade and two who would have been if they hadn't been expelled. Back then we called them stoners. Long hair; t-shirts with their favorite rock bands; jeans that looked like they'd been slept, pissed, and shit in; no personal hygiene; standard stoner wear. If they could manage leather jackets, combat boots, and decorative chains then they were the shit in their scuzzy little circles. I knew these guys by their faces but not their names.

They were assholes, and I tried not to familiarize myself with assholes.

One of them, tall and as awkwardly built as a scare-crow, with the complexion of a sausage pizza and the ugliest set of choppers I've ever seen on a kid his age—huge and crooked, yellow deepening to brown—spun her book bag by its straps, winding up for a throw that would send her books flying. Another held her from behind, twisting her arms behind her back, dry humping while she struggled to get away. The others stood by and laughed when the bag flew into the air, scattering her books, folders, and papers from there to hell.

I was running toward them without even having decided. It was automatic.

When I was still half a block away the book thrower pressed in on her from the front, squashing her between him and his arm-twisting friend. His hand drew back, swung forward. I heard the *whack* as it connected with her ass.

She screamed again, began to cry.

Then I was only a few feet away and closing fast, the time it had taken me to close the distance blotted out by anger so hot it burned memory away.

Scarecrow boy put a cupped hand over each of her small breasts and squeezed them, laughing merrily.

He was the alpha of the pack . . . the priority. The guy holding her from behind, short but built like a side of beef, was the beta. The other three, the ones on the side-lines cheering, were only gammas, to be ignored until they forced me to notice them.

They noticed me then, the dog without a pack, the nomad, but were too slow calling out.

I grabbed the alpha by the back of his shirt and yanked him off her, pitched his skinny ass into the air like a javelin. He yelped in surprise, screamed when he hit the ground.

Beta shoved the girl aside and came at me bellowing, his arms wide, leaning toward me in his balls-to-the-wall banzai charge. Guys who charge you like that never expect you to stand your ground. What they expect you to do is panic and run away, and they're usually right. I surprised him by meeting his charge with a ready fist.

It squashed his nose, split his upper lip wide. Blood sprayed impressively, but he didn't so much as whimper. He hit the ground in a boneless tumble, wisely deciding to sleep through the rest of the fight.

The girl sat where she'd fallen on the sidewalk, her arms crossed over her chest, her face a deep red and tears still leaking from her eyes.

I noticed her only in passing. She was out of my way and that was all that mattered. I turned my attention to the last three standing, the gammas, and found them running. The fight could have been over then, but I didn't want it to be. I wouldn't be satisfied until all of them were on the ground.

Before I could go after them a fist hit me from behind, connected with the back of my skull, and for the first time in a long time I was the one on the ground. The pizza-faced scarecrow of an alpha was up again, and the fucker was strong.

While I was on my knees, blinking away the stars, an arm slipped around my neck. It was a scrawny arm with scrawny muscles like steel cables. It choked the breath from me while the fingers of his other hand wound into my hair and held tight.

The alpha's chokehold was too strong to break, so I took hold of his narrow arm with both hands and broke it instead.

He screamed, it was the loudest, highest-pitch sound I had ever heard, and he let me go.

There was another of those black moments, then I was kneeling over him on the asphalt, holding him up by the front of his filthy Motorhead shirt. His face was bloodied, his eyes dazed, his consciousness already floating away like an untethered balloon, and my fist was drawn back for another punch.

"*Stop it!*" It was the girl, the nomad with the bloodied ankles. Their victim. "Just stop it! You're hurting him!"

I felt her tiny little fists rain blows down on my head, shoulders, back; and give me a little credit, I was able to stop myself from responding in kind. I had at least that much control of myself.

What I did was lower my fist and release his balled up shirt. His head thumped the ground and I saw consciousness shocked back into him. He didn't try to fight me off, just stayed put and bled.

Good boy.

What I did was turn to her and say. "I was *trying* to hurt him."

She gave me a look of pure loathing. It was like a slap in the face, bringing me back to my senses. The black rage faded and left me kneeling over the bleeding and newly demoted alpha dog, feeling stupid and sick with violence.

"*You didn't have to go that far,*" she screamed. "*They weren't going to hurt me!*"

She stood over me screaming, her little fists clenched at her sides. She was a brave little thing. I found that inexplicably adorable.

"They *were* hurting you," I said.

She held her ground, glared at me, and I knew if I touched Scarecrow again she would jump on me without hesitation.

So I stood up and stepped away.

She held me with her adorable, hateful glare for another moment, then turned her back on me.

"You're as bad as they are," she said, and started gathering up her books. Then, as if to prove beyond any doubt that chivalry was dead, and it was probably a woman who killed it, she said, "Go away!"

CHAPTER 10

It was a six block walk from the log yard to my cabin, three south, three east. I moved as quickly as I could without running, Trouble seemed to be resting easily under his cage's shroud, and I didn't want to get him going again. He gave the occasional click with his beak, but was otherwise silent.

What I wanted was to lock myself inside, set the alarm, go to bed. I'd settle for a change of clothes and my own guns if they were still there. I kind of doubted it, I simply don't have that kind of luck, but it was worth a shot.

But I needed to be careful, I needed to be smart. They could be waiting for me, somewhere on the block, hiding in the backyard, maybe inside with my change of clothes and guns. If I was smart, I would have skipped the detour home. Hell, if I was smart, I would have ditched the bird.

And to prove just how smart I am, I arrived at Port Drive and stopped for a moment to consider the dark little crackerbox cabins, the silent street and empty yards, then went on.

I found my front door still open but the lights turned off.

Lucky me, since those fucks took my keys along with my phone.

If anyone was inside waiting for me they would probably expect me to stop and reconsider my course, to examine the logic that had led me back here. It's what a sensible person would have done. But it was my home dammit, and I felt I had every right to be stupid in it.

I decided to approach the problem from a different angle.

If there is someone waiting for me in there, I reasoned , the last thing they'd expect is for me to just walk on in like they weren't there.

Yeah, that should throw them off nicely.

So thinking, I walked inside without hesitation.

There, that'll teach 'em!

I set Trouble's cage down just inside the door, put my right hand over the butt of the Beretta in my waistband, fumbled for the light switch with my left.

I was almost disappointed to find the room empty.

Luckily, my disappointment was short-lived.

I checked the bedside table for my guns; both gone, no surprise then the closet. Whoever had gone through here hadn't bothered with my clothes. I peeled off my sweat-and-dirt-caked t-shirt and selected one of my baggiest Hawaiian shirts, dark blue with bright yellow Hibiscus blooms. Very subdued, a good *blending into the crowd* shirt.

I was pulling it off the hanger when the toilet flushed from behind the thin partition wall.

"Oy, Simon!" The voice behind the thin wooden wall

was unexpectedly . . . British. "Whatchu come back for? You already nicked all the good stuff!"

What?

The bathroom door flew open and the man with the unexpectedly British voice stumbled through, half-tripping over his own feet and still yanking up his pants with one hand. His other hand clutched a familiar black portfolio. It was unzipped, hanging open, the pages fluttering from the rings that bound them. A photo slipped from one of the inner pockets and fell to the floor.

He'd been reading my Redwolf files on the shitter, checking out the crime scene photos, maybe jerking off to them.

I wanted to shoot him for that alone.

His *Sniveling Shits* tank top was vile with old sweat and grime. I could almost see a stink-cloud blooming from him. Lank black hair hung in front of his face. He flipped it back with a jerk of his head, saw me, jumped with surprise.

"You are one fuck-ugly Indian!"

I dropped my shirt and pulled the Beretta.

He'd succeeded in pulling his pants up but forgot to zip them. His hands flew up in the universal gesture of *I give up don't shoot me,* and the pants slid back down around his ankles.

"No offense mate," he grinned wide, showing a set of choppers like old crooked headstones. "It suits you! The scars . . . the face . . . very rugged!"

He gave me a thumbs up with one of his raised hands. The other still clutched my Redwolf files.

"Who are you and what are you doing here?" I thought it was a fair question and a good starting point.

"Oh, this and that," he said, unhelpfully in my opinion. "Boss says hang about for a few hours and take whatever I fancy . . . make it look like the bloke what lived here got robbed."

"The boss . . ." I said, indicating that I would like to hear more.

"Yeah . . ." he seemed to fall asleep on his feet for a few seconds, then twitched back to attention and began to speak again at roughly the speed of light. "Weren't nothing much good here but I found something manky to read . . . can I put my hands down now . . . hey, Simon's back!"

"Terry, you are the dumbest motherfucker alive." The voice was almost casual in its contempt, and came from directly behind me.

Before I had a chance to reassess the situation something cold and hard pressed into the center of my back. I was beginning to wonder if the Hibiscus shirt was worth all the extra trouble.

"Fuck off," Terry said, not to me but the voice behind me. He sounded honestly hurt.

"Drop the gun or I'll shoot you," Simon said.

"You forgot to say Simon Says," I said.

"Simon Says," Trouble squawked from his cage.

Terry jumped again and spun in amusing half-circles looking for the new intruder. His feet tangled in his dropped pants and he fell on his face. The portfolio flew, scattered more photos and pages, slid under the end of my bed.

Simon turned toward the closet and the muzzle of his gun left my back. "Who . . . ?"

I jabbed blindly with my elbow and grinned as I felt it crunch his nose. It made a very satisfying sound.

I turned in time to see him stumble back out through the open door.

"Puck, puck, puck," he shouted through the hand clamped over his gushing nose, then pointed the gun in my general direction and fired.

The slug flew wide, blew a chunk out of the bathroom wall instead of my chest wall. I didn't give him time for a second shot. I grabbed hold of his head, twisted my fingers through his short hair for a good grip and brought it down hard on my raised right knee. It crunched like a cockroach under a boot's heal. He dropped to the floor, twitched and flailed enthusiastically for a few seconds, then stopped.

Shit!

I hoped I hadn't killed him, I'd already made one corpse that night, but was afraid I had. All the shit I'd read about serial killers, and I'd read a lot about them, said that murder was more than just an acquired taste, it was addictive. The more you did it, the more you wanted to do it again, and again, and again.

I already had enough bad habits. I didn't need to add killing to them.

Terry was gone, slipped out the back door during the excitement and vanished into the Paradise Valley night.

I made the Beretta safe again and stuck it in my pocket. I slipped on my fresh shirt, transferred Candy's photo and the IDs into its breast pocket, gathered up my Redwolf stuff and zipped it back inside the portfolio. After a moment's consideration I decided to bring it with me. The stuff inside it was too important to lose, Gina had risked too much getting it to me to leave it laying around for Finke's fuckwad squad. Then I vacated the premises before the gunfire drew the inevitable cops.

I wasn't sure whose side they would be on when they showed up.

And I brought Trouble with me. Little guy came in handy sometimes.

"Here comes trouble," the bird muttered moodily as I carried him away from the soiled sanctity of my cracker box home.

"Tell me about it," I muttered back.

I had to hide three times on my walk to the parking lot where my Ventura waited, the first two times barely a block away from my house, behind overgrown hedges in the unkempt yards of derelict houses, the second of which was hosting a loud and possibly illicit party. The noise got Trouble going again, but I hushed him and he was unexpectedly compliant.

I think I was beginning to grow on the little guy.

Both times the passing cars rolled by a little too slowly and the occupants showed way too much interest in what might be going on beyond their windows.

The third time was from a cop. I spotted the cruiser turning onto Port Drive a block and a half away and hid in a mostly empty dumpster at a construction site. Climbing into the rank steel box roused Trouble again, but I calmed him with another whispered hush. Again, he repeated the hush and was silent. I watched the cop car's slow approach through the partly raised lid and hunkered down in the phantom stink of garbage long departed as it rolled past.

It could be worse, I thought, and almost immediately it got worse.

The sound of the cruiser's engine didn't fade as it passed me by, and a slamming car door confirmed the new depth of the doo-doo I was currently standing in. Dealing with Finke's cadre of losers and junkies was one thing, almost fun. But if this cop belonged to Finke I was looking at a professional strength complication. The sound of hard-soled shoes clicking on blacktop grew, then stopped directly in front of my aromatic sanctuary. A tense moment passed, and the lid began to lift.

Hoping like hell this wasn't one of the good guys I was about to clobber, I grabbed the intruding hand and yanked the man it belonged to inside with me.

The commotion inside the big steel box was loud but short-lived, and a minute later I climbed out with Trouble's cage swinging from my left hand and the portfolio tucked snuggly under my armpit. The right I kept free in case I needed my pilfered police Beretta. As I walked away I heard the police cruiser's radio give a short burst of static, then a crisp female voice broke the uneasy silence.

"Possible 10-71 . . . 1300 block of Port Drive . . . all units respond."

Yep, the time to get gone had officially arrived.

CHAPTER 11

I traded the seedy solitude of Port Drive for the slightly sleazier late night bustle of Main and continued toward my ride at as brisk of a walk as I could manage. I didn't run, nothing says *I'm doing something illegal, please arrest me* quite like a giant Indian running with a birdcage under his arm. Even walking I drew more attention than I was comfortable with, but the passing pedestrians confined their attention to guarded glances as they hurried past me. Mostly it was the cage they were looking at. Two cop cars rolled past a minute apart, no lights or noise. Happily they ignored me, and I returned the favor. The other passing drivers showed no interest in me at all.

As I think I've said before, there are advantages of being an ass-ugly seven-foot-tall Indian. When folks encounter you on a dark sidewalk they will *usually* respect your privacy. I think I also mentioned the disadvantages. All of Finke's friends would have my description by now, and if I did pass them I would be hard to miss.

By Fifth Street the traffic was thicker and the sidewalks dotted with loitering scumbags who looked even more suspicious than me. A baby-faced young gangsta gave me a lingering look as I passed him, but made no immediate move to follow.

I reminded myself that not every low-life in Paradise Valley belonged to Cameron Finke, and hoped I wasn't making another wildly inaccurate assumption.

By the time I reached the parking lot Trouble was getting irritable again, and no amount of hushing would shut the bird up.

The parking lot was fuller than when I left it, my car lost in a chaos of beaters and hotrods belonging to the Paradise Valley nightlife. I wondered how many of these cars belonged to Finke's guys, and decided not to worry about it. With luck I would blend into the low-grade chaos, people in groups, pairs, or alone, moving between the store and their parked cars. If I couldn't blend in, I was reasonably sure no one was going to cap me right out there in front of everyone.

The smart thing to do would be to watch me, then follow.

That was okay with me. I could shake a tail. I've done it before.

I made it to the Ventura without incident and set Trouble down by the rear tire, out of view of the lot's general population.

I dug in my pockets, it was habit, and remembered my keys were gone. My keys, my cell phone, and, I realized with a burst of anger, slapping at my rear right pocket, my wallet.

"Motherfuckers," I grumbled, crouching down to retrieve the hidden keys inside the wheel well. They were there, safe rattling inside their magnetic box. Ignition, trunk, and house.

I unlocked the driver door, tossed the portfolio on the front passenger seat. I was reaching for Trouble's cage when I saw the man from behind, only a few yards away and closing the gap between us with long, urgent strides. The baby-faced gangsta I'd passed a block or so back.

"Hey man, that's my bird you got there."

A group of passing teenagers slowed to rubberneck, a few of them grinning in naked anticipation. They smelled a fight.

I did too.

The guy paused for just a moment when I turned to face him, my face elicits that reaction more often than not, then moved forward again, arms held out wide, a challenging pose, the silly posturing of a semiprofessional thug. The guy was very white, light brown hair and pale eyes, but spoke with an exaggerated Hispanic accent. His pants were baggy, showing a few inches of dirty white boxer shorts, his baseball cap tipped at such a crazy angle I wondered how it stayed on.

"Where'd you get my bird, man? I think you and me should go for a ride." His hands came down and the right one dipped into the pocket of his filthy green jacket.

So much for doing the smart thing, I thought.

I waited until his hand went into the pocket, then stepped forward and punched him in the mouth.

In the interest of full disclosure, I have to tell you how much I enjoyed it. The look of disbelief on his face as he registered my fist coming at him—clearly he didn't expect such a large guy to move so quickly. The way his thin lips busted open, the spray of blood, a few of his teeth breaking off at the gum line. The thud he made as he hit the pavement spread-eagle.

It was all very therapeutic. The high point in an otherwise shity night.

The gun bounced out of his hand and skittered across the blacktop toward the loitering group of teens, a few of the boys shaking their fists at the sky and cheering as if they'd landed the knockout punch.

Their exuberance vanished at the sight of the punk's weapon, and the young men's girlfriends, clearly the brains of the group, hauled them away by the arms.

Most of the remaining rubberneckers went about their business and I bent to scoop up his gun before more people could see it and cause a commotion. Then I bent over him, palming the gun's ejected clip, emptied the chamber, dropped his piece onto his chest. The gun's appearance almost guaranteed a visit from the cops, and they might as well have something to do when they arrived.

The gun was another 9mm, the same model as the one I'd liberated from the walking tattoo's corpse. The ammo wouldn't fit the Beretta I carried but I wasn't going to leave this fuck-stick with a loaded weapon, not when there was a good chance I'd be running into him again that night. I hoped he wouldn't have a chance to bother me again, that he'd be picked up by one of Paradise Valley's good cops before he woke up, but as my long gone mother used to tell me when I was still just a little reservation kid, *Shit in one hand and wish in the other*. My best plans have a bad habit of going wrong for me. It's just my luck. I *knew* which hand would fill up first.

I squeezed Trouble's cage onto the floorboard of my

car's front passenger seat, adjusted the Beretta so it wouldn't shoot my pecker off if it discharged accidentally, and fired the Ventura up.

The old green beater was ugly but could outrun most street rods in the valley.

I pulled out of my space, carefully avoiding the snoozing baby-faced thug, and went to find another of Finke's snoozing thugs, hoping the guy would still be where I'd left him earlier that night.

I drove a block past Finke's street and pulled over at Riverview Park, only a half-block from the Goodwill donation drop and just out of sight of Finke's place. I waited, scanned both sides of the street as far as I could see, watched for pedestrians, busybodies, cops. I waited until I was sure I was alone, then waited a bit longer. I rolled my window down and listened for signs of life. Nothing.

That part of town was unusually still, even for this time of night. Maybe all of the usual nightwalkers and patrols were concentrating on Port Drive and the port district. Maybe they were hiding behind the trees in the park or out of sight around the corner of the mini-mall, waiting for me to show myself.

Maybe I was just being paranoid. Probably I was being paranoid.

I decided it was time to shit or get off the pot.

It turned out that the street was deserted.

I stepped out of the car, lit a smoke, walked casually through the park, glancing toward the donated clothing bin, then Funke's place, but only quickly, and as if they were only of passing interest. There were no snoozing drunks draped over the clothing bin. Containing my disappointment to a single hushed expletive, I turned and crossed the street. Wouldn't hurt to have a closer look.

This turned out to be the right move, which brought my average for the night up considerably. I hoped it would be the start of a new trend, hope in one hand, shit in the other, but didn't quite dare to congratulate myself. I was still in a world of shit.

The man was still passed out, still snoozing off a spectacular drunk, but he hadn't rested easy. At some point in the night he'd pulled himself deeper into the clothing bin and lay there still, curled up within the four-by-four foot confines like a dog in a kennel which it has outgrown. One hand was tucked deep under the elastic waistband of his sweatpants, kneading away at his crotch like a worry stone.

Another furtive look, feeling like a man trying to look in a hundred different directions at once, I bent over the bin and hauled Sleeping Ugly from his bed of secondhand clothing.

Then I recognized his face and almost laughed out loud.

Maybe my luck was turning.

The man passed out in the donated clothing bin, one hand under his cheek and the other down his pants, was my runaway pusher from the night before, the one whose girlfriend had tried to cook my nuts.

Phil Shepard.

The coming interrogation would now be more than just a necessary evil. It would be an enjoyable one!

He didn't waken during his rough relocation, only extracted the hand from his pants, and began to paw blindly at my face.

I resisted the urge to drop him back inside and scram. I cringed, thinking about the variety of germs, filth, and general nastiness that blindly groping hand might be spreading over me like smegma over a Ritz cracker.

Once this was over I was going to take a very long, very hot shower.

Once out of his hole, the guy hung from my arms like a smelly, snoring rag doll. I gave him a little shake to wake him up. His head rolled from one shoulder to the other. His mouth flopped open, disclosing a set of horror-show choppers and a shining line of drool.

"Asshole, wake up." I gave him another, slightly rougher shake.

He groaned, farted, smacked his lips. His right hand fumbled with the elastic of his sweatpants, sought the refuge of his crotch.

A few cars passed Second Street on the main drag, a block down from my Ventura, one exiting the bridge, not Redwolf Bridge but the old blue one that crossed from West Paradise Valley to East, one entering it. Somewhere several blocks away a horn honked and someone chirped their tires.

It was time to blow this part of town for someplace safer.

Bending down to drape one of the man's arms over my shoulders, I carried him along toward my car. The toes of his shoes scraped along the sidewalk, making a noise that seemed to echo loudly down the still street.

I made small talk with him, idle chat, hoping to project

a casual air to any passing car or peeping busybody. Just a guy helping a drunk buddy back to his ride, or a designated driver executing his duty. There were no keys or wallet in either of his pockets, but a cell phone deep inside one pocket bounced a little with each step.

More cars passed by on the main drag, but none turned in my direction or slowed to rubberneck.

I dumped him in the rear seat, relieved him of the cell phone, hurried to the driver's seat.

I started the Ventura, was about to make a U-turn back to the blue bridge, my next destination firmly in mind, when Phil's phone rang.

I shifted back into park and picked up the phone.

The front screen lit up, Incoming Call, and below that the caller's name.

Cameron.

After a half-dozen rings the Incoming Call faded and the display informed me that Phil had missed several calls, all from your favorite inconsiderate fuckwad and mine, Cameron Finke. An icon appeared at the top of the screen to let me know there was voice mail.

I was *very* interested to hear what Cameron had to say.

CHAPTER 12

The traffic through East Paradise Valley's main drag was much busier, almost brisk, but it was a different kind of nightlife. The kids of East Paradise Valley consisted mostly of yuppie spawn masquerading as street trash. A lot of teens and twenty-somethings dressed down to some fashion designer's conception of *street*. No wonder the real street trash west of the river laughed at them. The hookers and pushers were real enough though, and very obvious. They were the ones who looked like they actually belonged on the street. I didn't know how many ties Finke might have on this side of the river so I turned off Main at my first opportunity and threaded my way through the mostly deserted commercial streets.

The river was a kind of dividing line between the classes in Paradise Valley. The middle and upper-middle class tended to settle east of the river, the lower class, like yours truly, on the west. The notable exception to that rule was Snob Knob, former home of the late Candice Reynolds, AKA Candy Roche. Snob Knob was so far removed from the grungy downtown that most didn't count it as part of the West Valley.

The West Valley's seedier elements did good business with the yuppie spawn of East Valley but didn't tend to linger once business concluded. Hanging around rich kids for too long can be a real downer when you're not one. Even classless scumbags have feelings.

Now that I was on somewhat safer ground it was time to cool my heels for a few minutes. I had a few calls to make, starting with Candy's business partner, Honey Beloi.

I aimed the Ventura away from downtown, up through the sleeping residential streets, toward the suburban sprawl that overlooked the downtown.

Toward my port in the storm.

I remember mentioning that my uncle was quite the entrepreneur, but I think I only touched on about half of his ventures. He has a half-stake in a dozen other small enterprises, including a large block of storage units near the airport, up in the highland portion of East Paradise Valley known locally as The Heights. The half of ABC storage that he owned was the actual storage units, the land belonged to a local toss-pot who had inherited it but didn't have the business sense to do anything with it. The guy's first attempt at business was a restaurant, his last a nightclub that did a slow business for almost a year before he lost his liquor license, something about the bartender, his stepson, admitting underage girls and doing naughty things with them in the stockroom.

Uncle Higheagle loathed the man, but he never let violent hatred get in the way of a good business arrangement. The landowner wanted to make a living without working, Uncle Higheagle didn't want to have to buy that particular piece of land, only use it.

And good old Uncle Higheagle, he made it work. What his partner hadn't been able to fill with people, Uncle Higheagle filled with all their crap.

I didn't have much to do with this particular venture. Every once in a great while he'd call on me to clear out an abandoned unit, just throw up a few yard sale signs on the outer fence and leave the gate open and the bargain hunters swarmed like flies on yesterday's breakfast. Uncle would take enough of the cash to cover the unpaid back rent on the unit and what was left over was my bonus. I did some odd maintenance around the place and hosed the dust and cobwebs off the rows of long tin buildings every spring and fall.

The pay for my work at ABC Storage was permanent use of a double unit at the far end of row C, my office. It had a bay door and a regular door. I furnished it with a sofa, a smallish desk with a rolling office chair, and an often used coffee pot sitting on a mostly empty file cabinet. It was like Finke's garage but without the hookers and bad music. I'd thought about setting up a computer but decided against it. Hours stuck behind a computer screen was one of the things about my old life that I didn't miss.

The anxiety that followed me all the way from Redwolf Bridge began to settle as I neared the top of the 17th Street grade into The Heights and the airport came into view. The airport was a small two-terminal job with a half-dozen ticket counters, a couple rental car counters, and a coffee stand. During the daytime, traffic in and out of the airport is just this side of deadly. But the terminal closed between ten in the evening and six in the morning, so late night traffic was light. Once I turned past the airport and onto the meandering two-lane road that wandered toward the landfill, shooting range, then out to the shit-kicker boonies, there was none.

A mile later I rounded and turned the corner at the far side of the fenced in airfield, and my home away from home came into view. Another fence, and behind it four long warehouse-like structures.

On the backseat Phil began to groan.

I stepped on the gas, pushing well past the thirty-five speed limit. I wanted to be on the other side of that fence before he came around.

Phil began to mutter as I slowed, thumped his head against the back of my seat trying to sit up when I turned the corner onto ABC Storage's short drive, muttered sweet nothings as I rolled my window down and punched my pass code into the security panel.

The fence was electrified and topped with razor wire. Signs posted around the perimeter warned off potential trespassers, threatened them with fines, imprisonment, death. Even more convincing was the occasional smoked bird or squirrel. A larger sign on the gate informed potential burglars of the closed circuit security cameras posted strategically to capture every square inch of the property.

With a click and a hum the gate began to slide away. A few seconds after I passed it by, turning parallel to the storage units, it slid shut.

My guess was good and bottled in now. Even if he got away from me he wasn't getting out of ABC Storage.

"Wha . . . who the fuck are you?"

Phil poked his head between the headrests of the front seats, and I clobbered him.

"Aw! Fuck . . . my nose!" *Buck . . . by dose!*

"Sit still, man, I'm trying to drive."

"Fuck you!"

"Don't be such a baby."

"You broke it!"

I didn't bother replying. It wasn't broken. He was just being a pussy.

His phone rang again.

"Hey man, give me my phone back."

"Nope," I said.

"It's my fucking phone, man!" His voice grew louder, more strident with each exchange. "Gimme the phone man, I need it!"

"Nuh-uh."

"Who the fuck are you anyway? Did Cam send you after me?"

Interesting, I thought, and opted to answer with silence.

"Did he?"

I turned down my row, popping the glove box open and digging for the remote.

"Ah shit man . . . ohfuckohshit!" The man's panic sobered him.

Very interesting, I amended.

I held my silence. The guy was building up to a fantastic monolog. I saw no reason to interrupt.

I found the remote, pushed the button, and the bay door on the furthest unit slid upward.

My guest saw this and began to panic in earnest.

"Jesus Christ man, I didn't do nothin!" He began to climb between the seats again, grabbing at my shirt.

I half-turned in my seat again to feed him another knuckle sandwich, then had a better idea. I popped the glove box open and withdrew my favorite new toy. A short yellow wand with a pair of sinister looking brass prongs on the business end.

He was half over the seat now, his sweaty hands trying to get a grip on my throat. He grunted and thrust forward against the back of my seat as I gently applied my brakes.

I feared for the Ventura's upholstery.

I shrugged him off like an ugly jacket and gave him a sharp prod with his girlfriend's Wasp.

He didn't like it much more than I had, but that was okay. I was starting to enjoy myself again. I knew it probably wouldn't last long so I savored it and gave him another quick zap.

He flopped back against the rear seat screaming a high soprano and began to rave, blithering in a language that was half English, half fear.

"Do you want to live?" I tried to think of this question as a non sequitur rather than a threat.

There was a long pause, during which I reached my unit and swung the Ventura wide to pull inside. A motion sensitive flood lamp lit my way.

"Are you going to kill me?" Scumbag or not, the fear in his voice made me hate myself a little. I had to remind myself that this gentleman's friends had already tried to kill me.

"Only if you make me," I answered with complete sincerity. I hoped he'd read the most sinister of possibilities into my response—*cooperate with me, tell me what I want to know, and you might walk away from this*—but the truth is that I'm not a killer, at least not of the cold-blooded variety.

Well, there was the one time, but there's some back-story I haven't shared with you yet regarding that. If you knew it I think you'd probably understand.

I coasted to a stop inside the empty half of the storage unit, the half that served as a garage and auto shop, shifted into neutral, and killed the engine. I turned to regard my guest, and he looked up at me from the floorboard with naked fear, then shock as he took in the face that not even a mother could love.

"*You*," he said, and seemed to sink a little further into the old car's well-worn carpet.

He remembered me.

I was touched.

The bay door closed with a bang and he cringed at the sound, closing his eyes against it.

At last, he opened his eyes again, and looked up at me.

"I'm sorry. I'll go back to jail now if you want."

CHAPTER 13

An expert interrogator I'm not. I don't have the heart for it, or, as it turned out, the supplies. What I've always lacked in preparedness though, I make up for in resource-fulness.

Or, as Uncle Higheagle sometimes says, *Boy, you don't plan for shit, but you sure can fake your way out of trouble.*

One furniture dolly with squeaky wheels, one full roll of duct tape, and three ratchet straps later, I was ready to begin.

Phil stood strapped to the furniture dolly like some particularly scuzzy work of art, The Stinker, maybe, instead of The Thinker. Bound to the dolly at the chest, waist, and knees, ankles taped together, his hands lost in a ball of silver tape, my guest was as cozy as he was likely to get.

I began with coffee, for me, not him. It was the next best thing to actually being able to go home and sleep.

Phil bitched and moaned pretty much non-stop. It had been a good quarter-hour since I'd had to hurt him and it seemed prolonged substance use had fucked up his short-term memory. Or maybe he was just born stupid. Once I stepped back into his line of sight his recall kicked in and he mellowed out a bit.

"I thought you said you weren't gonna kill me." He managed to sound petulant rather than fearful. His demeanor was dour, his gaze accusing, his bottom lip pooched out like a child who has encountered his first injustice.

Not fair was the story his face told, unintentionally amusing, but in no way productive. I resisted the urge to remind him that life wasn't fair, thanks in large to assholes like him and his boss.

"I said I wouldn't unless you made me," I corrected him.

If anything, the pout hardened on his face. His eyes told me clearly what he'd like to do to me if he wasn't busy being tied up. He reminded me of the kind of parking lot tough-guy who likes to pose and threaten, posture and lunge, but who is never quite able to free himself from his girlfriend's restraining grip.

"What do you want?"

"I want you to explain in one hundred words or less why Mr. Finke might possibly be . . ." I paused for a moment, appearing to consider my next words carefully, in reality giving Phil a few seconds to reflect on his situation and his transgressions. If he thought Finke had sent me to punish him for something, he had probably done something worthy of punishment.

"Unhappy with your services," I finished.

He swallowed. His petulance was gone. We were back to fear again.

"You do work for him." He looked ready to weep.

"I want you to be perfectly honest, perfectly frank. I want you to assume that Mr. Finke already knows." I spread my arms wide and grinned, as if to say *Why else would I be here*, "Remember, one hundred words or less. Feel free to use whatever words you have left to apologize."

Phil, as it turns out, had been a very bad boy.

His confession actually went quite a bit longer than a hundred words, but I let it slide. The more the better, I thought. Skimming drugs and money for personal use was only the start. Phil's main job was to keep his ears to the street and make sure Finke knew all the vitals of his competitors, and his lucrative sideline was funneling information on Finke's operation to those competitors, small-time guys trying to stay unnoticed while working the same territory.

Phil had been running that scam for a few years without getting pinched by Finke or squashed by his side-line customers, which meant he was either extremely smart, or extremely lucky. My vote was for lucky, and I think he felt the same way. He behaved like he'd expecting something like this for a while.

He was giving me some solid information on Finke's organization in the mix; names of connections and clients, the particulars of at least one company belonging to his aunt that he used to launder profits. I wasn't sure if he'd given me enough to build a case on, but he'd certainly spilled enough to get the feds interested.

And it was the feds I needed.

All of it while I stood off to the side, just out of his peripheral vision, recording the session with his cell phone's video camera.

When he at last came to the apology portion of his confession I stopped recording and saved the file.

"That's good enough," I said, swinging my chair back in front of him and taking a seat. "I'm sure your boss will find it very educational."

Confusion dawned across his face, but he seemed to shake it off with minimal effort. He had more pressing concerns.

"You gonna let me go now? Was that the deal? You think Cam will give me another shot?"

"Not going to let you go, but I'm not going to kill you either, so you're still ahead of the game."

Phil's sullen look was making a comeback.

"As for how Finke's going to react when he finds out you've been fucking him, there's only one way to find out."

Sullen made a hasty retreat, and confusion once more slipped neatly into its place.

I opened his cell phone's recording feature and played back the first few seconds of his confession.

Phil listened and watched with growing confusion, thoroughly failing to produce the expression I most wanted to see. I decided I didn't have the time to wait for it, and helped him along.

"I don't work for Finke. Tonight I'm working for me."

And Phil finally produced the emotion I wanted to see. It was immediate, and satisfying.

Big deal, you might say. *Butch pulled a fast one on a guy who spends his nights in a Goodwill donation bin.*

Satisfaction is a rare thing. I take it where I can get it.

"Ah, fuck me!"

"Yes," I agreed.

"Why would you do that, man?" He looked close to tears. "What did I ever do to you?"

I declined to answer that question on grounds that he was in no position to compel me.

But now that our interrogation had evolved to the point where I ask my real questions, I found myself lacking any real questions to ask. Phil had already answered all the good ones.

I drained my coffee, thought about getting another cup, and a question did occur to me.

"Does Honey Beloi work for Finke?"

"Go fuck y'self." The parking lot tough guy had made his comeback.

I opened Phil's cell phone, checked the memory, and selected one of Cameron's missed calls.

"What'cha doing? Gimme my phone back. Let me outta here!"

"Cameron's been trying to get hold of you for a while now. I should give him a ring. Let him know you're doing okay."

"Hey . . . no!"

"I bet he'd find our interview . . . illuminating."

Silent. Sullen.

"Does Honey Beloi work for Cameron Finke?"

Finally, grudgingly, "No. She works *for herself*, just like *you*."

Fantastic, now the sore loser was putting in an appearance.

"She fuckin' hates him. That's why we always use Candy."

"Where does she live? And don't tell me you don't know," I added, sensing that he wanted to be a pain in the ass. "It's your job to know shit like that."

"Man, whoever you are, you should stay away from Honey. After tonight she won't matter to your business, whatever it is, one way or another."

Phil had just confirmed what I already knew.

"Where does she live?"

"I'm telling you man, it's probably already too late. She knows where Candy was tonight. When Candy doesn't turn back up she's going to start asking around. Cameron's gonna to get rid of her before she can start shit."

"Where?"

"Fuck it!" Something in his face, his frustration, made him look halfway bright. Made me wonder if maybe I was the dummy between us. "She lives in the studio apartments above that spic restaurant downtown. The one with the big fucking hat."

I nodded I knew the one.

"But if you get pinched man, you don't say a thing to Cameron. I didn't tell you nothin!"

"If I get pinched, it'll be a very long time before anybody finds you." I grinned, began to pull tape from a second roll on the arm of my chair. "You won't have to worry about Cameron anymore."

I'm a cup half full kind of guy.

Okay, that's a lie, but I digress.

And before he could make too much of a fuss, I unwound half the roll around his mouth, and pushed him into an out-of-the-way corner next to the desk.

The bad-boy corner, the perfect place to consider what a bad boy he'd been.

CHAPTER 14

My first impulse was to call Gina White, my old acquaintance in the FBI, the one law person I knew I could trust. I searched the contacts menu for several seconds before I remembered this wasn't my phone. Since I couldn't remember her number I called the only one I could remember, my Uncle Higheagle. No answer. Either he was asleep or out of range. I hoped for the former but thought the latter was most likely. He told me he might be away for the rest of the weekend, which probably meant somewhere so off the path that the wildlife needed permits to graze, and forget cell reception. A camping nut was my uncle. I waited for his voice mail then briefed him on my situation, one hundred words or less, then redialed and sent him Phil's confession.

If my predicament wasn't solved by the time he made it back to civilization then it would probably be too late to help me, but I could at least die with the satisfaction of knowing that Finke's days as Paradise Valley's Scumbag-In-Chief were numbered.

Next I called Honey, who was in his contacts list.

The force was not with me.

After three rings I got her voice mail, and it was not at all what I expected. No sexy come-on, no purred invitation to leave a message with a return number, no promise that she'd give me a good hard spanking if I promised to be a bad boy. Just a simple monotone voice, a computer's voice, telling me to leave a message at the beep.

I've don't like talking to machines, I'm always afraid they might talk back, and I wasn't sure a recorded message was the way to go. The situation being what it was, semi-complicated and deadly, I thought it required a slightly more personal touch.

Hi there . . . sorry, no, I don't require a hand job today. I just wanted to let you know your friend is dead at the bottom of the river and some bad people are on their way to get you. Probably they'll rape and kill you, maybe even in that order . . . who am I? I'm the repo man.

Yeah, so the personal touch probably wouldn't be much easier but I hung up without leaving a message. I'd give it a few minutes and try again.

I wondered how many goons Finke had working for him and how many he could call up in an emergency. How many were closing in on Honey. How many were out looking for me. Too fucking many I thought.

When there is no way to know for sure, always assume the worst. It's the only safe assumption there is. I also thought he'd have most of them out looking for me, since I knew they were after me and was already on the run. If I was lucky they'd be concentrating their efforts west of the river. Honey probably didn't have a clue yet, wouldn't know anything was wrong until they came knocking on her door.

Unless she was out working, or already dead.

Cup half full, I reminded myself.

If she was still alive they wouldn't bother with a trip to Granite Rock, they'd take her at her apartment, catch her sleeping, eating or fucking, and put one in her skull before she could make a fuss. With Candy in the wind she'd look really good for Honey's murder. A couple of whores got into a fight over money and one, quite possibly with her own growing rap-sheet of drug and prostitution offenses, killed the other and ran for it. Simple.

I was making assumptions again, but I felt comfortable with them. Exotic dancers work at clubs. Hookers post their services on craigslist.com and skirt the rules by calling themselves Exotic Dancers. As for Candy's imagined police record, she was a junky, and junkies tend to get busted doing stupid junky shit. It's all part of the glamorous junky lifestyle.

I checked up on Phil one last time and found him still nicely trussed up. He had no choice but to behave. I poured myself a final half-cup of coffee and drank it in a single gulp. I was going to need the caffeine.

I kept some extra clothes and a ratty pair of coveralls in a locker next to my workbench. I found a light jacket inside it, old, almost the same shade of green as my old Ventura. It was summer's ass end and still hotter than hell even this late in the night. Not necessarily light jacket weather, but the jacket had two inner pockets, one for my *borrowed* Beretta and one for the Wasp.

I could quit worrying about shooting my dick off now.

I turned off the lights before opening the bay door and hopping in the Ventura . . .

And noticed Trouble's cage still sitting in the passenger seat. The bird was silent, still, finally asleep. A short internal debate ensued; bring the bird or leave it?

I decided to bring it, not because I was starved for conversation, I wasn't, or because I thought it'd have something useful to say, there wasn't an insult it could throw at me that I wouldn't already have heard. I brought Trouble along because I thought having the bird with me would go far toward convincing Honey I was telling the truth.

If it got to be too much of a pain in the ass I could still toss it out the window.

I called Honey twice while I was on the move, once only a few miles from my office, just before dropping down the short grade from the East Valley Heights toward downtown, and a second time as I passed from the East Valley's old brick monstrosity of a high school, the dividing line between the sleepy residential and lively business districts. I got her voice mail both times and hung up without leaving a message.

Then, just as I entered true downtown, still alive and crawling with East Valley yuppie spawn, she called me.

When the phone rang I assumed it was Finke again, trying one last time to contact the shithead this phone belonged to, but I checked the caller ID anyway, and was surprised to see the names Candy/Honey glowing up at me. Distraction free driving is the law of the land in

Washington State, but after killing a couple of guys, stealing a car and a cop's gun, and kidnapping another man all in one night, I decided the distracted driving law could go fuck itself.

I answered the phone with a tentative, "Honey?"

There was a pause, a silence that seemed to stretch on for a long time, then, "Where is Philip?"

Her voice was everything I could have hoped for, more than making up for the bland computer voice on her messaging service. She had a thick Slavic accent, Russian, Serbian, or Ukrainian. From the same part of the world as Finke's illegal ammunition. Her English was not hesitant or awkward, just a little slow. It was probably her second language, but I guessed she'd been here long enough to learn it well. Her voice was as light as smoke, smooth as silk, and sweet as, well, sweet as honey.

I imagined a real life Natasha Fatale, posed on a leather sofa wearing nothing but stilettos and gloves.

I found myself momentarily speechless.

"Who is this?"

"Sorry, Phil is tied up at the moment." The pun was unintentional. "Listen, we need to . . ."

"No, whoever you are, you listen to me." There was real anger in her voice. No fear or rage, anger's awkward cousins. Her tone was cold, controlled, and shot through with a blue-steel thread of real hate.

"You tell that dripping prick I am not interested in doing business *or* pleasure with him." She was not a fan, apparently. I hoped it would make my work that night easier. "Tell that Drugstore Cowboy to get out of my building. He may have Candy hooked through the cunt but *I* have standards!"

Honey's perfect English blurred in her fury, wilting at the edges and becoming something even more exotic, a porn-grade Natasha Fatale.

Something near the end of her angry speech startled me out of my fascination with her exotic voice.

"Finke's in your building?"

"Yes!" She was shouting now, "down the hall by the elevator."

I shushed her, eliciting an angry caw from the other end of the line.

I scanned the upcoming intersections and pressed the accelerator a little closer to the floor.

"Don't let him hear you! Don't let him know you know he's there, and don't even think of leaving your apartment." There was a pause, during which I considered what I was about to say next, wondering if it would sound too melodramatic.

Honey said nothing, waited.

"If he sees you, he'll kill you."

More pause, I could hear her breathing, then, "Who the hell are you?"

I gave her a heavily abridged version. We didn't have time for the full story. I was only a few blocks away.

By the time I was finished and enduring another of her uncomfortable silences I could see her Main Street building only a block away. I pulled over alongside the grimy picture window in front of Dr. Rock's Records, a local mom and pop music place that still did a good business but hasn't actually sold a *record* in well over a decade. It was just out of sight of Honey's flat and anyone who might be keeping an eye on it. Then I walked back, turning left down the narrow lane behind the block of Main Street buildings.

I stopped there, safely hidden in the shadows, and scoped out the fire escape on the backside of Honey's building.

"Sit tight, Honey, and don't panic. I'm coming for you."

Sit tight, honey, I'm coming for you.

I still dream of saying those words to Daphne as she calls out to me over her cell phone, and tearing up the road to Redwolf Bridge, to find them before the monster could hurt them. In this dream my girls are there, but I can't see their faces, only blank pink, featureless flesh where their faces should be. The monster is there too, just a shadow in human shape. I run it down, smash it into puffs of black vapor, but somehow I know it'll come back. I haven't killed it, only frightened it off for a while.

I reach for my girls, and even with no faces I know them by their clothes, their postures, the way they hold hands.

That's when I wake up, alone in my little cracker box cabin with its bare walls and no love.

I have worse dreams, scarier dreams, nastier dreams, but this is the *cruelest* dream of them all.

CHAPTER 15

Finke's eclectic crew of fuck-wits had Honey surrounded.

There was a man dressed in black, crouched on the second story platform of her fire escape, one man standing below it, and another lurking in the mouth of the narrow alley between her building and the one I was hiding behind. There were probably more inside her building, and probably stationed at the building's front entrance. Maybe more milling around in the streets trying to blend in, but maybe not.

I thought I was probably still their first priority, the one who'd seen too much and gotten away. Honey was a sitting duck. Finke wouldn't blow his load, metaphorically speaking, on her. His hard-on was still aimed at me.

He couldn't know that I knew about Honey, and even if he had known I don't think it would have changed his direction. He just didn't know me well enough to guess the depths of my stupidity.

I took a deep breath, trying to settle myself. It didn't work.

"Fuck it," I said aloud, though very quietly, and put my plan, such as it was, into action.

———

I walked back to Main Street with my hands in my coat pockets and my head down, scanning surreptitiously for any familiar or suspicious faces in the fluid crowd. None was familiar, most suspicious.

My plan sucked, and give me a little credit at least—I knew it.

The Mexican restaurant was closed, its windows dark and shuttered, but next to it was a recessed entrance and another door. Behind that door a staircase led up to two or more apartments, one Honey's flat. A man stood inside the recess, blocking the door like a bouncer at a nightclub. He never got a chance to notice me coming, I turned down the narrow little alley toward my first target. If I could take this guy out before the other two blocking her fire escape saw me coming my plan *might* actually work.

There were no shadows to creep stealthily in and nothing to hide behind. I couldn't scale the wall for a ninja-like pounce. There was no way to reach him unnoticed so I just plunged in. I did keep my head down though. I didn't want him seeing my face until it was too late.

He saw me coming and tensed.

I put a finger to my lips in a silent hushing gesture and waved for him to come to me. I didn't vary my pace, didn't show any apprehension.

Hey buddy, you can trust me. We're on the same team.

He hesitated for a moment, gave a quick peek around

the corner at his fellow slimeballs posted at the fire escape, then rushed to meet me at the alley's halfway point. His pace was hurried, his posture still tense.

I stopped and lit a smoke, held it out toward him with my right hand. My left went back into the jacket pocket, wrapped around the stubby handle of my new favorite toy.

"What's the fucking holdup?" He spoke quietly but his irritation rang loud and clear. "I know he wants to keep it quiet but I ain't got all fucking night." He reached for the offered smoke and froze when he saw my face.

Yep, this guy at least had heard about me, even had my description. I was a very popular man that night.

He yanked his hand back, probably to reach for his gun.

I jabbed the Wasp into his chest and gave him the juice.

There were a few sparks and a bit of crackling, a low buzzing grunt from the guy getting the juice, but the Wasp was obligingly low key.

He flopped back against the brick wall, stiff as a wedding night prick, his feet tapping a frantic rhythm against the littered alley blacktop, his arms working like pistons beneath spasming shoulders. He looked like a speed freak trying to do The Robot.

Very entertaining stuff, but I didn't want to kill him, and I did need to get moving. I cut the juice and caught him by the front of his shirt before he could fall, eased him gently down to the ground.

As much as I enjoy the sound of an asshole hitting pavement, I didn't want it to carry.

I checked his pockets and found pretty much what I

expected in one of his rear pockets. I made sure it was safe and added it to my growing collection. I looked toward Main Street to make sure I didn't have an audience, then punched him once in the face to make sure he didn't get up for a while. There was no joy in it, punching a guy while he was down and out, but I didn't want him coming around and fucking up my plans.

I recognized the man below the fire escape as one of Finke's partiers from earlier that night. Tall, wiry, mostly bald, what little hair he did have around the sides and back of his head was long and pulled into a ponytail. His attention was focused overhead at the man crouched outside Horey's rear window.

After a quick look back to make sure that the alley guard was still snoozing, not creeping up to thump my head for me, I poked my head out of the alley, toward the man under the fire escape, and called out to him.

"Psst!" Cliché, I know, but effective. The guy twitched amazingly and cut a fart that echoed down the quiet back street. He spun his sweat-shiny head, illuminated a sickly yellow by the nearest street side lamp, to and fro, his greasy stoner's braid swinging. His hand dipped inside his leather vest when he saw me.

"Aw, knock it off," I hissed in a ridiculous parody of conspiracy. 'Come on, I got a message from Cameron."

His hand paused on its journey to his gun. He looked surprised and confused.

"Come on," I said again, and gestured wildly with both outstretched arms.

"Okay . . . okay." His hand returned to his side, and with one last upward look, left his post.

I backed into the alley and waited for him to appear. After a few moments he did.

"What?" He sounded pissed. His expression was one I recognized, the put-upon expression of the professional slacker, always first in line when the free booze and drugs were on tap, always first to slip away when the party ended and it was time to clean up.

The clever line of text on the shirt he wore beneath his vest, *I'd Rather Be Fucking*, seemed to confirm my impression.

If Finke had given this reluctant footman my description, it seemed to have slipped his mind. He regarded me without doubt or caution.

I put my index finger to my lips in a shushing gesture then looked back over my shoulder. The alley was clear. So was the small bit of Main Street it faced.

When I turned back to the reluctant thug I saw him rolling his eyes and fidgeting in place.

I grabbed his ponytail, and before he could as much as grunt in protest, used the pink dome of his head as a battering ram against the brick wall.

The wall held. His head proved too soft.

One hit was all it took, he hung by his ponytail like a bloody mannequin. A life-size Halloween prop.

I considered giving him another, more to satisfy my bad mood than anything else, and decided it would be unsporting. I relieved him of his gun, eased him to the ground.

Two down, one to go.

The guy on the fire escape was a bit smarter than the last two.

I left the concealment of the alleyway and approached the fire escape without trying to hide. I could be stealthy as hell on the ground but once I started climbing he was going to hear me. There was no way around that, so why even try. I thought trying to be sneaky and failing might be a great way to get dead.

"Hey!" I sprinted out from the mouth of the alley and waved at the guy. "Come down. Time to go."

This guy was much more into his role. He was also very quick. He had his gun out and pointing at me before I knew he meant to draw.

"Stop."

I stopped, raising my hands to shoulder level as my boot heals skidded on pavement. "Whoa . . . hey!"

"Who are you? Where's Scooter?"

"Scooter's gone, man. We're finished. I'm supposed to drive you back." I hooked a thumb back over my shoulder, a vague gesture toward the mostly empty parking lots down the street.

"I didn't hear anything," he said, dropping his voice almost too low to hear. He glanced over his shoulder at the curtained window into Honey's flat.

"He was quiet," I said. "C'mon man!"

"Shhh!" Sharply. Another nervous glance over his shoulder. Then he looked at me again. "I don't know you."

Shit!

Glancing back and forth between the window and me, undecided, then, "Get up here, I'm calling him."

He kept his gun on me while I climbed, fumbling his

cell phone from his front pocket with his clumsy left hand.

I clanked and banged my way up.

"You clumsy fucking oaf, be quiet."

The climb was short. When I lifted my head up over the second-floor platform, I was staring down the barrel of another of Finke's crappy 9mms.

I could see by the sudden widening of his eyes that Finke had given him my description, and that he *had* remembered it. "Holy shit!"

I could have tried to bare-face my way out of it, but didn't see the point.

"You're the guy?"

I smiled, shrugged. "I guess I am."

He moved back a few steps. "Up here. Be quiet or I'll shoot."

I complied, and staring down the barrel of his gun felt a familiar and dreaded emotion begin to fill me up, a kind of reckless abandon, not quite suicidal, but not far from. It's the gleeful insanity that I'd fought off earlier that night, that sometimes overtakes me in potentially fatal moments.

The fact that I have had enough potentially fatal moments for this gleeful insanity to be familiar says something about my run of luck.

"What the hell are you grinning about?"

"Been a funny kind of a night," I said, suppressing the laughter that built up behind my chest.

I rose another step up through the hole in the platform, leaning my ass against the short railing, settling the rung of the ladder into my boot's arches, bracing my heels against it. I lifted my open hands to shoulder level again, a gesture of surrender.

He crouched a few feet in front of me, knees spread wide for balance. He kept his narrowed eyes on me and his gun pointed at the tip of my nose, almost close enough to bump it. "Don't move."

"Not going anywhere, boss," I said, and some of that insane good cheer escaped in a snicker. It made a sound I hoped he would somehow mistake for fear, maybe even the precursor of tears, but I didn't count on it. Finke's men had mostly proved themselves to be morons, but a snicker doesn't sound like anything but a snicker.

I could not quite help the smile that curled my lips though. As hard as I tried I couldn't bend the corners of my mouth back down into a more properly humble shape.

"Go on and smile all you want, hatchet-packer," the guy said, returning my smile with a sneer. "Cameron's gonna wipe that smile right off your caveman face."

I flicked my eyes from his face, up and over his shoulder at Honey's window for just a second.

The goon's eyes widened slightly and he turned toward the window. As he did his gun wavered left of my nose. Not far, only a few inches, but enough.

I let go of my barely held laughter, it exploded from my mouth like silly string vomit. Feet planted firmly on my supporting ladder rung, I leaned forward.

He was facing me again in the short time it took me to reach out, trying to bring his gun back in line with my nose, but he was too late.

With my left hand I gripped the narrow wrist of the hand holding the 9mm, and gave it a hard turn in a direction it was never meant to go. There was a nauseating crunch, toothpicks snapping and guitar strings letting go with quick pops, as the complication of bones and tendons in his wrist stretched apart. Then I cupped his crotch with my right hand, first lifting, then squeezing until I could feel his balls squash in my hand beneath the denim of his pants. His high shriek became a falsetto siren.

I could still hear my own laughter over his Mickey Mouse wailing, but just barely.

His 9mm clattered to the steel grate.

His eyes, squeezed into threatening slits only seconds before, were open wide now, bugging out in a cartoonish expression of shock and pain. He squawked out one last time before running out of breath, a sound that reminded me of the bird, hopefully still asleep in the front seat of my Ventura, and I lifted him over my head.

This is too much, I remember thinking. *You're not going to do it are you?*

Apparently I was. I tossed him into the air two stories above the empty back street and watched him fall.

He was silent on his way down, seemed he'd wasted all his breath in the initial scream atop the steel grate platform, but he made a very large sound when he landed, a deadly sound two parts *crunch*, one part *splat*.

Shouldn't have done that, I thought, ascending the ladder's final steps and mounting the fire escape, but sometimes when that dangerous hilarity overtakes me I just can't help myself. I do unnecessary shit.

I paused on the fire escape for a few seconds, crouching, though at my height crouching doesn't do much good, to survey the quiet back street.

No one came running, no crowd of inconvenient rubberneckers materialized around the broken body.

Now would be an excellent time to get the fuck out of here, I thought. *It's not too late yet. Chivalry's dead, stabbed through the heart by a woman and left to stink. Get back to the office and sit tight until morning.*

Good advice. There's a time to fight and a time to run and hide, and I knew what time it was. Yeah, excellent advice, and as usual it appeared I had no intention of following it Cursing myself for the moron I knew I was, I shambled to Honey's window and gave it a tap with my knuckles.

CHAPTER 16

I learned the fine art of running and hiding when I was still just a little kid on the reservation. It's a skill I've held on to in the years since. Practice makes perfect and all that shit.

A few days after administering that legendary beating to two of Sacajawea Middle School's most feared and hated students—the Scarecrow and his beta, the walking side of beef—that old skill came in handy once again. Scarecrow's big brother and his pack of dedicated potheads, elder statesmen of Paradise Valley's stoner community, caught up to me on my walk home from school.

I was stupid, I should have anticipated it. I should have at least changed my route home to make them work a little harder for it. It had been a few years since I'd had my ass thoroughly kicked for me and I was getting sloppy.

My bad, as they say.

Elizabeth Trout was taking a new route home now, I

suppose my total absence made it even easier for her to ignore me, or maybe she did smell a little payback coming our way. I never asked her and she never volunteered the information. Either way she wasn't there when the old Trans Am rolled up beside me. I was glad she wasn't there. As much as she hated me I don't think she would have been able to walk away from it. In fact, I know she wouldn't have.

It was the Smokey and the Bandit car, black with gold trim, so '70s you almost expected to see a disco ball hanging from the rearview mirror. I loved the car. I was not as pleased with the faces I found staring out of it at me. One of them was Scarecrow, eyes and nose swelled out of their usual shape, lips split and crusted with scabs. I recognized him immediately, and I could see he recognized me too.

He twisted clumsily in the front passenger seat and pointed me out with the index finger of his left hand. His right hand and the arm it was attached too were in a sling resting on his lap.

"Dat's h_b," he shouted through his ruined lips. *That's him.*

I turned and ran, vaulted over a short fence into the nearest yard, past a fake tombstone draped with fake cobwebs. RIP, it said.

"Get him!"

A quick peek over my shoulder confirmed my worst suspicions. The backseat passengers, greasy blonde hair with black denim and combat boots and a chubby guy in army khakis, leapt out to chase me on foot, and the Trans Am sped down the road and around the corner.

"Shit!" Chubby leapt the fence but caught a foot

between the short plastic pickets, pinwheeling his arms before plunging headfirst into the fake tombstone. The gray Styrofoam split in half and Chubby ate grass. *"Fuff!"*

Combat boots passed him without a look back, and I faced forward again.

Looked like I was taking the long way home.

The side yard was narrow, I had to duck to pass beneath the low limbs of an apple tree. I reached up and plucked one as I ran.

"Hey!" A fat, middle-aged man wearing a purple polo shirt and the silliest pants I've ever seen, purple and gold diamond patterned, paused with his golf putter raised in mid-swing. *"Get off my property you bastid!"*

That was the plan.

The backyard fence was taller than the front but not too tall to get over. Just as I was about to hoist myself over it the familiar Trans Am came to a screeching sideways stop on the next street, waiting for me.

Shit!

I dropped back to the grass and dodged Combat boots just before he plowed into the fence.

"Hey! Hey!" The old guy was waddling toward us now, brandishing his putter like a club.

I started back the way I'd come and Chubby appeared in the side yard to catch me, swatting the low hanging limbs from his face. I pitched the apple in my hand like a baseball and it burst open on his forehead. He grunted in surprise, stumbled back a step, tripped and landed hard on his ass.

Movement in my periphery, colorful movement. I turned in time to see the old guy swing his putter at me.

I jumped back, the putter clipped my shoulder. It stung like hell but I was still standing.

The old guy tottered on the edge of his lost balance, and good boy that I was, I lent a steadying hand as I rushed past him, toward the fence and the next yard over.

Combat Boots was after me again, and the old guy paid my kindness back by giving him a good whack in the gut.

"You bastids get outta here." He took another clumsy swing, missed, shook his putter in the air. "Call'a cops Margie! Call'a cops!"

Good idea, I thought, but wasn't waiting around for them. I hoisted myself over the fence and landed in a crouch on the other side.

No golfers in this yard, just a scattering of lawn tools and a pile of leaves. I spied a rake leaning against the fence and grabbed it, waited. A few seconds later a pair of hands grabbed hold of the fence top and Chubby's face popped up between them. I brought the rake handle down on top of his head and he disappeared.

Pleased with myself, I took a step back and laid the rake down in the grass, the tines poking up where my own feet had landed. I scattered the leaf pile over the rake but didn't pause to admire my handiwork. I showed them the back of my head, what dear, dead old mom called my *good side*, and ran like hell.

There's no way it'll work, I thought. *Never*.

But as I turned the corner around the house, back toward the street where they'd rolled up on me, I heard a *whack* and shout of pain. I couldn't help myself, I stopped to have a peek back.

Combat Boots had come down square on target and

stood dazed, the rake's tines under the toes of his boots, the handle standing straight up against his stunned face. A narrow line of blood trickled from his forehead.

I resisted the urge to cheer and bolted around the side of the house.

The street was empty, but not for much longer I was sure. I sprinted through the yard, more Halloween shit, a straw man hanging by a noose from an elderly oak, another fake tombstone, a plastic hand reaching up from the ground.

I love Halloween. So festively morbid.

Home was in the other direction, but so was the Trans Am, so I ran on.

I cut through yards and kept off the streets as much as possible, I was threatened and chased off by home owners, my legs grew rubbery with exhaustion. I wanted to go home. I hadn't seen the Trans Am. I decided it was as safe as it was going to get, and got back onto the side-walk, walking—I was all out of run by then—toward home.

Daylight retreated and I continued, marking every street sign I passed and adjusting my course from block to block. I also kept an eye on the cars that approached. No Trans Ams. My tension eased with every block, then every step when I was down to the last few. I was going to make it.

Now I just had the next day to worry about, and the next after that.

Never mind one day at a time.

Uncle Higheagle was going to be pissed, I was beyond late, but at least I knew he wasn't going to beat the shit out of me.

And that was when they caught me.

I turned my last corner, Uncle Higheagle's big house in sight, and saw the Trans Am parked just down the road. The cab was empty.

Run, I thought, but never got a chance.

The driver, Scarecrow's brother it turned out, rose up from behind a row of trash cans, I turned and found Combat Boots coming at me from the other direction.

A hand clamped on my shoulder and yanked me within beating range.

I was big for my age, but they were at least five years older, bigger, and there were three of them. Then Scarecrow was with them and there were four.

I've taken worse beatings, and it would have been worse if Uncle Higheagle hadn't come to see what the commotion was.

I've taken worse, but it was bad enough.

I spent the rest of the week at home pissing blood and eating aspirin, and word must have gotten out because Friday after school the doorbell rang, and when I answered it I found a flower and a card on the doormat. Whoever had left it was gone.

It was from Elizabeth Trout, standard *Wishing You a Speedy Recovery* crap, and a short personal note scribbled below.

No, I'm not telling you what it said. I'm willing to share just about anything with you, but that is mine. You can't have it.

By the time I returned to school she was gone, her parents had pulled her out of the hormone charged madhouse called Sacajawea and sent her to a private school. I didn't get the chance to thank her for the card . . . or her message.

My point? Chivalry's dead . . . remember that and act accordingly. And if you can't take that advice, then at least learn how to hide better.

CHAPTER 17

The first I saw of Honey was a hand.

It was small, the skin milky white, the fingers long, dexterous, prettily tapered to long, narrow nails perfectly manicured and polished to a deep and decadent red.

It slid beneath the dark curtain, a movement both simple and sensual, and her fingers flicked the window's catch open.

Then it was gone.

I waited for a moment but the hand didn't reappear. I picked up the fallen goon's gun, the latest addition to my growing collection, and slipped it in my jacket's outside pocket. Honey might need it to defend herself.

If, I thought, *she even knows how to use one.*

I decided that her hand's brief appearance was the only invitation I was going to get, and pressed both hands against the glass of her window. It slid up easily just a whisper of sound and seated firmly into the top of its track. I lifted one leg and stepped inside, ducked as low as my lanky frame allows to follow it inside.

"Honey?"

I kept my voice low but didn't whisper. The long stretch of room I saw beyond the dark curtain appeared deserted. I stood where I was, one foot on the old shag carpet of Honey's flat, the other on the fire escape, bent painfully low with the arch of my back scraping against the bottom of the raised window, and let my eyes adjust to the darker interior of the room.

Not bad.

They'd transformed the pit of a flat into something stylish, comfortable. Tapestries covered the windows overlooking Main Street, an aged adobe wall and crumbling staircase overgrown with flowering vines, a high window overlooking a garden paradise sewn into cloth.

"Hey, Honey."

No answer.

I stepped the rest of the way inside and when the curtain fell in place behind me I saw that it wasn't a curtain, but another tapestry.

To my left was a small kitchen, what Honey undoubtedly thought of as a kitchenette, partially separated from the rest of the big flat by a folding partition.

"Psst!"

No reply.

I reached for my Beretta then decided against it. She was probably already scared. I didn't want her hysterical.

There was a narrow door to my left, open just enough to see the bathroom. Next to the bathroom another door was deadlocked and chained. Across from the bathroom another partition stood, blocking my view of a large piece of the room.

Only two places to hide, the bathroom most likely. It had a door.

The place was lightly furnished, a silk-draped futon, two squat armchairs with a coffee table between them, two floor lamps that threw more shadows than light.

A potted plant hung from the ceiling where a light fixture should have been. Its reaching vines crept across the ceiling, suspended by unseen wires or strings. Devil's Ivy. Fitting.

"Honey!" A little louder now. I didn't want Finke to hear me, but I had to risk it. Time was short. The bad guys were going to run out of patience soon and come busting in. If someone discovered Scooter and his suspicious friend, the cops were likely to show up soon as well. Maybe they would be straight cops, maybe not. I didn't feel like taking the chance.

My eyes had adjusted as well as they were going to. I crossed the room in a rush, ducking beneath the Devil's Ivy, pushed the bathroom door open.

"Honey?"

"I don't know who you are or what you want from me . . ."

I spun on the spot, my aching muscles moving with adrenalin speed, and saw Honey in the corner of the room cut off by the partition. This was obviously the part of their shared flat where she rested her pretty red head at the end of the day, whenever her *day* happened to end.

Honey sat, half reclined against the plush red cushions of a narrow wicker futon. Another small table beside her supported another dark lamp, a glass of something on the rocks.

Thick, silky red hair, flawless pail skin, full lips, red as cherries, shining like a wet dream. Her body, so perfect it was impossible not to stare, its shape not hidden by the short and filmy black dress that barely covered it.

The gun in her hand.

It was pointing at me.

Not one of Finke's crappy 9mms. I recognized the make and model from one of Posey's gun bibles, a .357 Glock subcompact, the extra four inches on the barrel having nothing at all to do with penis envy. A small gun that would make an impressive hole in whatever, or whoever, she shot with it, sufficiently suppressed that she could pop an intruder without waking the neighbors.

She looked relaxed, almost bored. The Glock looked far too comfortable in her hand, and that hand did not shake.

I, on the other hand, was shaking, partly in fear, partly with an uneasy emotion that was almost lust. One a little more than the other.

". . . but you have only thirty seconds to win me over, or I'm going to put a very large hole in you."

Why, goddamnit why, does everyone keep threatening to shoot me?

For the first ten seconds I was able to say nothing, and immediately following that I managed a grunt that sounded more like a fart than speech.

Honey's sleepy look hardened a little after the first ten seconds of silence. After the next ten seconds, her eyes began to widen in alarm, thinking that perhaps I meant to call her thirty-second bluff.

But I didn't think she was bluffing.

I have had people bullshit me before, and I've done the same to plenty of people, and there is one thing all wind-bags have in common. Big mouths and no balls. They specialize in big talk and cheap shots, calling the cops when you won't turn your radio down at night, or drop-ping an anonymous note to some douchebag's boss to tattle on him for abusing the company credit card or jerking off in the bathroom.

When it came to life and death most threats *are* bluffs, and when you call them on their bullshit they give them-selves away. They fidget, they stammer and stutter, they twitch, they sweat.

Mild alarm, or maybe it was only irritation, was as far as Honey's anxiety went. I thought maybe she was annoyed about the mess she was going to have to clean up if she had to shoot a guy for breaking in, probably with no good in mind.

She sighed.

"Could you move a little to the left? I don't want your blood to ruin my Trish Biddle."

I actually stepped to the left, not quite getting the sense of her words until I looked over my shoulder and saw another of her fucking tapestries, this one of a flapper in an open back evening gown. The picture reminded me of her, actually, including the flapper's hair, which was the exact same shade of burgundy as Honey's.

Holy fuck, she's going to do it.

I opened my mouth, presumably to speak, though I had no idea what I planned to say.

"The parrot's waiting for you in my car," I said, and felt a blush heat my cheeks. I'm not shy by nature, and I'm not easy to shame, but there was something about this woman that made me feel like a little boy.

For a second the look on her face suggested she was considering shooting me on general principles, then she lowered the gun a little, only a little. It pointed at my crotch now instead of my chest. Not a huge improvement.

I could feel my time running out, both inside this small flat and outside it. Finke's boys were sure to discover their downed scuzzballs soon.

"It's not a parrot. It's a macaw." This sounded like an often used line, her answer to a minor faux pas, but something that happened with enough regularity to annoy her. "Where's Candice?"

"At the bottom of the river," I said.

Her reaction was not what I'd expected, not denial, rage, or tears. Her brow furrowed, the corners of her mouth dropped into something resembling sadness, but that was all. She gave a little nod of acceptance and lowered her pistol a little more, kneecaps now instead of crotch.

Getting better.

"And he's come for me, so I won't tell on him." Now there was anger, in her voice rather than on her face, but I couldn't tell if it was directed at Finke or her dead friend. "I told her what kind of man he is but she kept going to him."

She swung her legs off her futon and stood. She was tall, near six feet, slender, curvy, the avatar of sexy. I felt something trying to stand at attention, wanting to point at her as she'd pointed her pistol at me, and I reminded Little Butch there were more pressing matters.

"What kind of man is he?" I'd managed to form a

pretty rock-solid opinion of him in the past few hours, but Honey seemed to actually know him. I didn't know if understanding the enemy would help but it couldn't hurt.

Honey looked at me, lifted her eyebrows, almost smiled.

I relaxed.

She has a very expressive face, easy to read, or so I thought at the time. I would learn differently by the end of the night. By the time this particular misadventure was finished I would come to realize that you only read what she wanted you to read, only saw what she wanted you to see.

Her expression then, bemused, then amused, suggested that I was being spectacularly ignorant, asking a dumb question.

"He's a wolf, of course. A wolf who looks like a man."

A knock sounded on the door then, and not a polite little knuckle rap. Someone on the other side meant business.

She turned from me to the door, then back to me. Her eyes raked me from top to bottom. "So tell me, big boy, how are we going to handle the big bad wolf?"

I told her.

She smiled, her pretty lips curving up to erase her anxiety, then those lips opened to reveal two rows of the most perfect and white teeth I've ever seen. That grin made her look a little crazy, and I was pleased to realize that Honey was no cowering little lamb of a woman, no fragile flower who would shiver her petals off at the first sign of danger.

"Butch, I think I like you."

The feeling was mutual. Boy was it ever.

CHAPTER 18

The knock came again, the knocker not realizing that Honey was already at the door and peeking through the peephole to make a positive identification. She withdrew the chain lock and sliding bolt, using the noise of his pounding to mask the click as she disengaged the lock on the doorknob, then backed quickly away into the deep gloom of her flat.

I had turned off the floor lamp, now the only light in the flat came from the lamp in her odd little bedroom. It cast narrow, slanting beams through the lattice top of the partition and made odd shadows around the questing vines of the Devil's Ivy.

"Come in, come in!" She called out in mock exasperation as she slipped back into the full glow inside her private corner of the flat, then laid back on the overstuffed cushions of her eccentric little wicker bed.

The knocking ceased, but for a few seconds no one came inside. For a second I could only wonder, then the flaw in my plan came clear to me. No doubt he'd tried the door and found it locked before resorting to knocking.

Did he smell trouble brewing? Did he sense a fast one in the making?

Almost surely.

Then he did open the door, I could hear the minute creaking of its hinges. There was a long moment of still-ness, perhaps ten seconds, perhaps more, then the door creaked shut again and latched with a resounding *click*.

From my hiding spot in the bathroom, crouched behind its cracked door, I saw Honey flinch at the sound, but she looked otherwise calm.

Good.

Maybe she hadn't seen the flaw in my plan yet. Maybe she hadn't realized I was no good at this kind of shit.

Then I saw a man's silhouette as he passed between me and the light, and tensed, keeping my gun trained on him, ready to resort to *plan B*, shoot and get the fuck out, if he showed his gun.

He didn't, not yet at least.

"Hi, Honey," he said, and I could hear a kind of jolly good cheer in his voice, laughter only barely suppressed. "Long time no see, darlin'."

Not Finke, I could tell by the voice even if I couldn't see his face.

"Not long enough." Honey's voice was even, calm, disdainful. "What do you want?"

"Hey, now," he said, hurt on the surface, amused underneath. "That ain't nice. I only came to talk."

She yawned hugely. "Then do it quickly and leave. I'm trying to sleep."

Pretty good, I thought.

"You know I wouldn't be here if it wasn't important," he said, sounding put upon, sounding regretful, the unwilling bearer of unhappy news. "It's Candy . . . she's had herself a bit of an accident and I thought you'd wanna know since you're so close and all."

"Really? Did she slip and fall on a needle again?"

"Something like that," he said, and now he had to work to hold the laughter back.

He seemed to be thoroughly enjoying himself, a condition I hoped to remedy very soon. I pulled the door open, slowly, and stepped out of the bathroom, closing the ten feet between us in soft, tippy-toe steps.

"You see, a horse bit her. Bit her good, but don't worry, I took care of her."

"And now you're here to take care of me too," Honey said, her voice still holding that uninterested tone. She yawned again.

His hand moved around the small of his back, toward a small bulge under the hem of his shirt.

"I wouldn't do that," I said, closing the remaining few feet in a single large stride.

His hand paused behind his back, his fingers twitching in surprise, and as he began to spin around to face me, I brought the butt of my gun down against his temple in a single, hard arc.

It made a soft, yielding thud, like a hammer hitting a pumpkin, the man grunted once on his way to the carpeted floor.

I smiled, slipping the piece back into my pocket. Turned out Finke's crappy 9mms were good for something.

I heard a thump behind me, an elbow bumping a wall

maybe, or the toe of a boot striking one of Honey's potted plants, and knew I was screwed. I tried anyway. Spinning clumsily on the spot, damn near tripping over my own feet, fumbling for the gun again, I found myself facing Musclehead.

He grinned at me; zircon studded gold grills glittered in the low light, making his grin something more mechanic than organic.

How had I missed those choppers before?

His smile was like the grill of some ugly old car, a muscle car.

I reached for one of the guns stuffed into my pocket, but too late. Musclehead's large fist looped around and came at me from the left before I could draw. I abandoned the attempt in favor of a good old-fashioned tactical maneuver. I ducked, just avoiding my second power-nap of the night as his bling-covered fist glanced off the top of my noggin, then sprang forward into him.

No one sucker punches me twice in one night!

I hit him with as much force as I could manage, but it was like trying to tackle a statue. He rocked back slightly when I hit him, and shoved back hard enough to send me stumbling. I lunged forward again before he could decide how to kill me and punched him in the stomach.

It was like punching a statue.

I shouted in pain.

He chuckled, grabbed me by the throat, began to squeeze.

I punched him in the stomach again.

He seemed not to notice.

His grip on my throat tightened.

The darkened room began to grow even darker.

I punched him in the balls.

He noticed that.

Musclehead let out a low groan of pain and seemed to shrink a few inches. His grip on my windpipe loosened, and I pulled in a painful breath.

I went for my gun again, pulled it free, but didn't get a chance to use it. He swatted it out of my hand, and before I could dig for another of my weapons he swatted me into unconsciousness.

When I came back no more than a few seconds had passed. I was on my back, the old floor cool beneath me, staring up at Musclehead's wide, shining grill. With the hanging tendrils of Devil's Ivy hanging above his head and Vincent van Gogh's Starry Night, another tapestry, of course, hanging behind him he looked like a strange monolith standing tall into some alien sky.

Transfixed by the image, I groped blindly for my gun, not finding it. I had others in my jacket, two or three now, couldn't remember for sure. I'd never get one out in time though, because the grinning monolith above me did have his. He seemed to take great joy in pulling it from the snug waistband of his shorts, pulling the hem of his Gold's Gym shirt up to free the butt, revealing a ripped abdomen that looked like something forged from iron and wrapped in skin.

"Fuck," I said. At least I think that's what I said. To be fair I was under a moderate amount of strain, so if my memory isn't one hundred percent clear on that one point, you'll just have to forgive me. *Fuck* would be a very close approximation at any rate, if not dead on.

What happened next was unexpected enough that it took me a few moments to register it properly. That sparkling grin exploded red, a bright supernova of a smile that outgrew the man's face. He seemed to forget about the gun in his hand, took a few stumble-steps in my direction, leaning down toward me as he did so, and I could imagine him thinking *fuck the gun, I'm gonna eat that sucka.*

Then he was falling over me, that great, gaping red smile expanding as it fell toward my own face. His eyes were no longer in their sockets, they'd popped out and swung from a thick gristle of tendons and optic nerves.

I smelled burnt powder, and my understanding finally caught up with my senses.

I tried to roll out from under Musclehead's falling body but wasn't quite quick enough. A second later I was covered by a heavy heap of slack muscle and the exploded, dripping meat that used to be a face. He'd landed on top of me in a sprawl, his limp arms and legs pinning me like the fleshy bars of some gruesome cage, the large hole that used to be his mouth covering my own. His eyeballs pressed between his cheeks and mine. One of them popped like a squeezed grape. His tongue fell across my lips like a large, slick slug.

It was like a prison rape scene with zombies.

I had the presence of mind to turn my face away before screaming, then I rolled his limp rag doll body off of mine and sprinted the half-dozen steps to the bathroom, slamming the light switch up as I entered it. Forgoing the small sink basin, I charged into the shower stall and bent, whacking my head against the old tile of the wall as I cranked the hot and cold taps simultaneously.

I'm going to have to get tested now, I thought, and puked like I've never puked before.

When I'd finished washing all the blood from my hair and face I turned the taps off and stumbled back into the living room dripping wet.

Still reclined on her wicker futon, her small, silenced Glock in one hand and a cigarette in the other, she regarded me with an expression caught somewhere between pity and embarrassment, the kind you get for someone else when you see them do something patently dumb. She shook her head.

"You really are not very good at this kind of thing, are you?"

After a few moments spent trying to master my gag reflex, I said, "Sorry, Honey. I'm learning as I go."

The guy I'd thumped into dreamland gave a feeble groan, then snored as if to say he was thoroughly bored with the night's business.

We went out the way I came in, and I led the way with my Beretta drawn. To my surprise, the coast was still clear. I didn't trust it, but it was either this or the front door, and we knew there was company waiting impatiently out there.

Honey followed me out, then down, her dress shivering around her thighs.

I was a good boy, I only looked up once. The most interesting thing I saw on my quick glance was a small holster, a simple rigging of cloth and Velcro, currently empty, strapped to her inner thigh.

I landed on the empty back road, my gun raised and ready. A moment later Honey was beside me.

"I hope you don't plan on leaving a trail of bodies for Finke to follow." Honey motioned to the broken heap of humanity bleeding out in the far gutter of the narrow street with the barrel of her Glock. "Your handiwork, I take it?"

"Naw. He slipped on a banana peel." Both hands free now, I pulled the Wasp from my jacket's front pocked and flicked the on switch. I liked it for close work, and I thought there might be a bit of that between where we stood below her flat window and my car, parked a block away.

"Lets go" I strode past her, then several paces beyond before I realized she hadn't moved. When I turned to see what the holdup was she stood, arms crossed, eyes narrowed, giving me a look that would have hurt my feelings under less deadly circumstances. "What?"

"Why should I trust you?"

Okay, so the girl had trust issues, and probably well founded.

I struggled internally for an answer that she might accept, and perhaps the pause in the conversation was answer enough to her. She raised the gun again, only a little. Not pointing at me, but all it would take was a single twitch of her hand and it would be.

"You're not inspiring confidence," she said, and backed away a step. "I can go my own way now. Goodbye."

"Honey?"

"Yes?" She sounded mildly amused, but skeptical.

Polite enough to hear me out but not stupid enough to actually believe me.

"Come with me or don't, but keep in mind I'm the one who didn't try to kill you up there." I thought about turning away and going it alone right then, probably would have been simpler, but gave her a second to think it over.

She regarded me with the same distrustful expression, arms crossed. Then she pointed her Glock at me.

"Drop!" She shouted, and I obeyed.

There was a single pop from Honey's Glock, then cursing behind me and the sound of retreating feet.

I rose to a crouch and spun, gun raised, saw the flutter of a shirttail at it turned the corner into the alley. He shouted an alarm. There would be more on the way now, and stationed between us and my car.

"This way," Honey shouted, and a moment later her hand clenched on my shoulder.

A head poked around the corner, eyes widened as he found two guns pointing at him, then popped out of sight again. "They're here! Tell him they're both here!"

"There will be more soon," Honey said. "Come with me."

I pined for my wheels. Cars really are wonderful things, able to whisk you safely away from countless bad situations—Thanksgiving dinner with the in-laws, psychotic blind dates, their disgruntled former owners, murderous thugs with poor personal hygiene and armor piercing rounds.

There's a lot to be said for a good pair of boots too. I used mine and joined Honey.

A half-block later I felt her hand close over my wrist

again and she pulled me off course. I saw where she was headed and balked. Another alley leading to Main Street. I didn't like it, and was about to say as much when the banging behind me started. Two shots, neither striking me, although they might have if Honey hadn't pulled me off course, but any bullet fired in my direction is a bad thing, to be avoided if possible.

"Hey, knock that off!" A shout from ahead stopped the gunfire, and was therefore not an entirely bad thing, but the man-shape that stepped from the shadows a moment later meant that we now had trouble coming from two directions.

Honey's alley was now officially the only route left. I allowed her to drag me into it.

"Stop!" Again there was pressure on my arm, and I could have plowed on anyway, maybe dragging her in my wake, but then I saw what she was looking at. A service door set inconspicuously into the brick of the old building. I stopped, but reserved the right to flee in panic.

"What are you doing?" I tested the knob, found it locked. I had expected nothing else.

"Shut up." Honey said, and shoved me aside.

I could hear running feet approaching at the back-street end of the alley.

Honey tapped on the door, once, twice, then a quick double-tap. A long pause, then once more.

"I don't think that's going to work," I said, and then four men appeared at the end of the alleyway. Four armed men. Armed, as I think I've said, with deadly body odor and deadlier armor-piercing slugs. The last bit in partic-ular is worth repeating.

I turned to the Main Street end and found three more

advancing toward us, Finke himself flanked by Tattoo's and Musclehead's replacements. I didn't like the looks of his new guys. They were a little too alive for my taste.

I looked at Honey, who was still facing the door expectantly, and to my surprise, the door opened.

I didn't need Honey to drag me in by the arm this time. I was very willing enough to take this new and unexpected detour, wherever it led.

CHAPTER 19

The door slammed closed behind us with a large sound, like a rusty gong struck by a rubber mallet, and I turned to find the strange young man who had let us inside sliding the deadbolt home. He was an interesting figure, short and bone skinny, dressed in baggy pants crisscrossed with chains. He wore no shirt, unless you counted the light chainmail draped over his shoulders as clothing. Every available surface was tattooed, gauged, or pierced. He had a thick head of long, dirty-blonde hair, all sticking straight up in foot-long spikes.

He turned, jingling as he did so, and his heavily modified face broke into a surprisingly welcoming smile.

"Honey . . . babe! I'm stoked to see your face in the place!" He began to bop up and down, as if dancing to a rhythm only he could hear. "You ready to party or what?"

She was too busy leaning against the wall, her eyes closed and panting with the night's exertions, to answer.

His eyes fell to the Glock in her hand, then to me, the Beretta in my right hand, the Wasp clutched in my left.

"Whoa, we like to party hard but not *that* hard."

Outside, fists began pounding on the door.

"*Open up, Honey. We don't want to hurt you. We just want the big ugly guy.*"

He regarded Honey again, and chuckled. "You've been a bad girl, haven't you?"

Still out of breath, but smiling herself now, Honey said, "Boswell, you have no idea."

"Time to get scarce," Boswell said, showing a remarkable lack of concern. He put a companionable arm around Honey's waist and guided her away from the door.

"Just a second," I said, and put the Wasp's brass contact pegs against the rattling doorknob. I pushed the go button on my favorite new toy and the scream on the other side lifted my mood considerably. High pitched, rising for a moment like the warble of a siren before it stopped entirely.

Honey shook her head. "Must you antagonize them?"

Boswell responded before I could. "Lighten up babe. A guy's gotta have *some* fun."

Boswell led us through an empty storeroom, long empty by the look of the place. Zero furniture, dust thick on the floor and mildew on the walls. It smelled like the inside of a dust-bunny's asshole. As we neared the other side a slight vibration hummed through the floor, then grew stronger. At the other side we passed through another door and onto the cramped landing of a narrow staircase. The vibration beneath my feet was much louder now, and the ratcheting electrical buzz of some aggressive techno music drifted up to gang rape my ears.

"I've been trying to get Honey to one of my raves forever." He turned and winked at her. In the low light of a flickering overhead bulb it looked like the salacious wink of a punk rock vampire. "I thought she'd bring a bit of class to the place."

"Absolutely," I said, following them with my head bent to avoid the low ceiling, although I thought he might have been more interested in her *ass* than her *class*.

Honey seemed to have picked the thought right out of my head. She turned around and favored me with a brief but withering glare.

To Boswell she said, "Sorry Boswell, but I'm only passing through tonight."

Passing through?

I had no idea where she was leading me, but at this point in the hilarity I was willing to follow.

"It's all good babe," Boswell said. "Maybe next time I can get you to hang around for a while."

They stopped at the bottom, before yet another damn door. The music pulsed and boomed on the other side. He turned back to me and had to almost shout to be heard. "My raves are the absolute shit . . . fucking all-star! We like to drop a little X and get a little naked!"

"I can only imagine," Honey said, now regarding the door with some alarm. She was probably wondering if she might be safer with Finke and his boys.

"Why imagine when you can *experience*," Boswell said, and pushed the door wide.

It was indeed an experience.

As I followed them through and pulled the door closed

behind us I wondered how much of this I'd be able to handle before having a seizure. Bright light pulses: green, red, blue, blinding white with a speed that was almost psychotic. The music was as frenetic as the lightshow. I felt like I'd just stepped inside a killer robot's head.

The people were all as . . . unique as Boswell, and it appeared that most of them had indeed been overtaken by seizures, or maybe possessed by disco demons. I saw faces in quick flashes of color, wild eyes, rag doll poses captured in the stuttering light; the too-relaxed *don't give a fuck* faces of the terminally stoned.

And many were indeed naked.

A girl with tiny hard-boiled-egg titties and orange hair spun through the crowd like a top, attempting to sexually assault everyone she came into brief contact with. A totally shaven guy with a giant eyeball tattooed on the pink crown of his dome sported a set of welding goggles and nothing else. He was moshing through the crowd with such enthusiasm that I thought his junk was in danger of hitting the floor and being danced on.

My moment of inattention was enough for the crowd to swallow Honey and Boswell. I stopped to search for them and unexpectedly found myself at the center of a gathering crowd. They encouraged me to join the fun by bumping me, rubbing against me. A playful hand, I'm not sure if it was male or female, found my crotch and began to squeeze.

I jumped back in alarm, collided hard with someone behind me, and was rewarded with a return bump and a hearty "*Yeaaahhhh!*"

Time to move, I thought, and did, scanning the crowd for Boswell's tall blonde spikes and Honey's sleek scarlet hair. The crowd did not part willingly before me, but no one seemed to mind my rough treatment as I shunted them aside. Then I found myself pressed against the naked top with the orange hair.

She stood about level with my chest, her head tipped back, looking up at me with wide, startled eyes. She recovered her enthusiasm for meeting new and interesting people and trying to copulate with them quickly enough though.

"*Whooo-hoooo*," she said, and threw her arms around me, clutching, grinding in time to the music.

"Quit screwing around," Honey shouted, pulling Orange off me and shoving her aside.

Orange seemed not to mind. She spun off in a new direction, presumably to find someone else to be naked with.

Tap . . . tap . . . tap-tap . . . tap, I thought, recalling the special knock that got us inside. I needed to remember that.

Like Boswell said, a guy's gotta have *some* fun.

Honey pulled me the rest of the way across the dance floor too quickly for another crowd to form around me, and on the other side of it we met Boswell again.

"*Where do you wanna come out?*" He shouted to be heard, but I had no idea what he was talking about.

Honey nudged me impatiently. "*Where's your car?*"

"By the music store."

Boswell nodded, but I couldn't tell if it was in response to me, or if he was just getting down with the beat of the new song that had just started, inspiring a round of cheers from the dance floor. They seemed very happy to have a new song. They seemed pretty much happy with everything.

Boswell led us along the basement's brick back wall to a large upended desk. He shoved it away from the wall to reveal a large, rough hole in the old brick wall. We'd have to crawl, but we could get through.

I was about to ask what was on the other side when Boswell reached up and put a friendly hand on my shoulder. "Go through and go left about a block and a half, then take the second left. You'll find your way out."

"Thank you Boswell," Honey said, and planted a lingering kiss on his cheek.

He grinned, blushed. "Anything for you babe. You sure you won't hang for a while? Your friends should be here any time now. We can party with them too."

"Not this time," I said. "We really have to split."

Boswell's smile faded, but he nodded. "We'll hold 'em up for a bit."

Then he turned back to Honey. "Maybe next time?"

Honey said nothing, only smiled.

Boswell nodded, as if he understood. Or maybe he was just picking up the beat again. Hard to tell.

"Wait for my signal, then run."

A moment later he was lost in the crowd again, and we crawled through the hole in the wall, into the darkness on the other side.

We dropped down a few feet to a filthy stone floor, and wherever it was, it seemed to be roomy enough to stand in, so I did, then fished the smashed pack of smokes from my pants pocket. Only a few left, but this might be the only break in the action I'd see for a while so I lit one, then held my lighter up like a torch to scope out the new surroundings.

A service tunnel, gas and water and sewer pipes servicing all of downtown. A thin scrim of greenish sludge clung to a channel in the concrete floor. Somewhere closer to the river it would lead to a pipe for pouring storm water into the river. Mostly it was just a narrow and empty space. I saw a storm drain leading up into the night just within the range of the flame's light. There would be more, set every half-block or so, and manhole covers too. Our way out.

"We're under the sidewalk," Honey explained unnecessarily. She pointed. "That way and take the second left."

"Nice," I admitted. I never would have thought of it.

I waited anxiously for Boswell's signal, whatever it might be, hoping that I'd be able to hear it over the ongoing party when the time came. A few minutes later we heard it, a shout that boomed above the noise like a war cry.

"Banzai!"

There was an answering cry from the dancers, then shouts of protest that were quickly drowned out by a new and even more obnoxious song.

Honey laughed, and we ran.

It was a short and dirty trip, hard to get lost in a concrete tube, but the dark slowed us down. We almost missed the first intersection in the dark, Honey spotted it in a slant of weak light falling from a storm grate. We slowed down so we wouldn't miss the second. Ten long strides after the turn I flicked my Bic again and saw the grime-coated rungs of an iron ladder leading up to a manhole cover.

I climbed, it was only a few steps to the top, and shoved the iron plate up and out of the way. The fucker was heavy. The sight that met my eyes on the other side of it was not encouraging. The service entrance opened up directly beneath a parked car.

My parked car.

"*Fuck!*"

"Quiet," Honey said below me. "They might be coming!"

So I said it again, quietly.

"Would you hurry up!"

"I can't." I jumped down so she could see.

"Well . . ." she seemed at a momentary loss for words, frustrated beyond her ability to express. She regained it quickly though, and expressed herself by punching me in the arm. "Crawl under it or something."

"Are you kidding me?"

She shoved me aside and began to climb. She slithered out under the Ventura like a snake, and a few moments later was looking down at me.

"Keys." I reached down and dug them out of my pocket and tossed them up to her.

While she shimmied out into the night I settled back and waited for Finke and his boys to arrive, or not.

CHAPTER 20

Sometimes you expect the worst to happen, and usually you'd be right. At the end of everything, of every life well lived, saints and sinners and normal people like us, the worst is waiting, and there's nothing we can do to stop it. That's what it means to be human. We're born in pain and grow in pain. No matter how hard we study or work or try to do what's right, even if we succeed in the best possible way and get everything in life we want, the end comes. The world swallows us up and shits us out.

Life is the ultimate dead end.

And deep down I think everyone knows it. Some just ignore it better than others.

So you expect the worst to happen, and usually it does.

But sometimes the best thing happens. Sometimes life throws us a prize we know we don't deserve.

Some take it for granted. Some *try* to earn it, *try* to deserve it.

Maybe the big guy in the sky only gives us these prizes so he can point and laugh at us when he takes them away.

I'm not convinced he exists, maybe only because I don't want him to. If he does exist then he's a bastard.

Shit, I'm turning prematurely cynical.

The best thing that ever happened to me was in college, when I was still just a hopeful young pup.

I was on the quad, on a bench, a drink from the campus coffee stand in one hand and open book in my lap. I felt very collegiate. The book was Vector Mechanics for Engineers. The drink was a large five shot mocha.

I expected to hate college. I enjoyed high school about as much as I enjoyed explosive diarrhea, but Uncle Higheagle had talked me into it, and it was good.

"Hieronymus?"

My happy mood hit the ground with a splat. A few passing coeds turned my way at the sound of that voice, one raising a hasty hand to cover her smirk.

"Hieronymus Quick?"

The voice was very distantly familiar. It would have to be. I'd put a stop to that *Hieronymus* shit years before. From high school on I was Butch.

"Yeah . . . that's me." I turned to face my unwelcome company—anyone who called me by *that* name was unwelcome—and lost the ability to speak for a moment.

"Oh my god! It's you!"

Yeah, it was me, but who was she? Why did she look so damned familiar, short hair so dark it was almost black, lightly freckled white skin, very pretty? The sight of her smiling face shocked the breath from me.

She took a step toward me, then hesitated. Her happy surprise wilted like a flower. "It's me . . . Beth Trout."

Trout. The name rang a distant but strong bell. I felt my pulse start to race, my heart pound, felt the zing of adrenaline, the body's way of taking the brain for a trip back in time. All the way back to the eighth grade and the sound of a scream, the sound of mean-spirited laughter. The thrill of rage, and my ungrateful damsel in distress.

The card left on my doorstep, the handwritten message that I'm still not going to share with you.

"Elizabeth Trout?"

She groaned, but her smile returned.

"Please, just call me Beth."

Beth was the best thing that ever happened to me, and the absolute best thing was that she kept on happening. It lasted for years, and every year it got better.

Until it got worse.

Things always get worse.

It's the only thing in life you can count on.

CHAPTER 21

I waited anxiously for a bunch of bad guys with guns to show up while Honey moved my car off the open manhole. I sent good vibes toward Boswell and his ravers. I jumped at the sound of the engine starting, then smiled as the rubber rolled.

Things were finally getting better. In a few minutes I'd be laying rubber and moving at roughly light speed back to the safety of my office, protected by a parameter of electric fence and barbed wire. Then we'd be safe until I heard back from Gina or Uncle Higheagle.

It was starting to look like I'd land with the shiny side up this time.

And as the concentrated roar of the Ventura's engine over the open manhole faded, the sound of heavy footfalls stepped from its shadow. They echoed in the tunnel, coming my way, and swiftly.

I grabbed the ladder and hoisted myself up, waiting for the last little bit of my car to clear the hole so I could escape. I saw bad going to worse a second before it happened and dropped back down the ladder before my rear passenger tire could complete the job that nature began and completely ruin my face. It thumped down into the hole as my feet hit the ground and started squealing against the rim as Honey stomped on the gas.

"Around there!" A shout from close, too close.

I had unwanted company.

God I wish I was at home sleeping.

Only one safe direction to go, away from the approaching footfalls, deeper into the tunnels.

Great, they can catch up and kill me when I'm good and lost.

With that in mind I turned and ran in the one direction they could never have predicted, and met them head on as they rounded the corner.

It was, as I've said, dark down there, but not perfectly dark. Some light fell down through the storm grates, falling in diffuse bars. I could see the dark man-shapes as they came skidding around the corner, and I was expecting them.

They *weren't* expecting me to be there to greet them.

I had just enough time to brace myself for impact.

There were three of them in the lead. The middle one ran face-first into my chest and bounced back with a grunt of surprise. I put my arms straight out and clothes-lined the other two. They went flying feet-first into the air and came down hard on the concrete floor. Guns flew and scattered across the ground, one discharging harmlessly down the empty end of the corridor.

The guy sprawled on floor of the main tunnel seemed to

be out of the fight for a bit. He didn't move anyway. The two laid out beside me were moving. I didn't like that at all. I bent down and grabbed each by the hair of their heads and lifted them from the ground. I found their groggy screams of pain pleasing but didn't really have the time to enjoy them. I smacked their skulls together and made them stop.

I knew there should be more, wondered where they were, but didn't have to wonder for long.

Bullets whizzed down the corridor in front of me, the wind from them brushed my cheeks as I stepped back around the corner. I drew my gun, aimed blindly around the corner, returned fire. In the brief muzzle flashes I recognized the man who'd bounced off my chest and lay sprawled on the tunnel floor.

Your friend and mine, the King of the Ass-Hats himself, Cameron Finke.

I sent more shots down the corridor, there were no screams of mortal agony, which I must admit is always a letdown, but I heard heavy bodies hit the dirt as they dove to the ground. I stepped out into their shooting gallery before they could rediscover their balls and grabbed Finke by the leg, dragging him back until we were safe behind the corner again.

In the sudden absence of gunfire I noticed that Honey was no longer revving the hell out of my Ventura to get the rear tire unstuck. In fact I didn't hear the Ventura at all.

She'd said fuck it and just kept going.

Smart girl.

Finke looked to be coming around. He began to squirm as I dragged him toward the open manhole. I decided I liked him better sleeping and punched him in the face until he did it some more.

His men were coming, the ones down underground with me were on the move again, running my way. I decided that if they were going to get me, and with my wheels moving fast in some unknown and unhelpful direction as they probably were, I was going to take this troublesome fuck out first.

I crouched down and held Finke in front of me like a shield, put the muzzle of my Beretta to his temple, and waited.

A few seconds later they were there, not the four I'd expected, but two. They took aim, saw the limp rag doll they called boss, saw my gun at his head, and lowered their guns.

"Make you guys a deal," I said. "Drop those guns and run back the way you came, and I won't put any holes in your boss."

They said nothing for a long moment. I couldn't see their faces, at that distance and in that lighting they might as well have been shadows, but their postures were expressive enough. They remained tense, unmoving. They did not ditch the guns.

Finally, one of them spoke.

"Yeah . . . that don't sound like such a good deal to me."

Up came the guns.

A shot rang out overhead, unexpected but not unwelcome. It was quiet after the continuous thundering crash of the past few minutes. Almost a whisper. One of the man-shaped shadows flew backward and thudded to the ground.

I aimed at the last one as he danced in place searching for the hidden shooter, and made him dead too.

This was getting ridiculous. I was in danger of losing track of the body count.

I looked up to see Honey hanging upside-down from the street above.

"Come on, big boy. What are you waiting for?"

Getting Finke up from the tunnel into the dark above took some doing, but I managed it with a little help from Honey at the topside. I emerged just behind him, dirty and sweating and in a slightly foul mood.

"What do we need *him* for?" Honey kicked him with a shoe that was completely inappropriate for the night's adventures. I think it was a pump. It was black and shiny and barely covered her foot. At least it wasn't a stiletto. She began to tap the other one against the blacktop, impatient for a reply.

Finke began to snore lightly in response to the assault.

"Bargaining chip," I said. "And I want someone handy to take responsibility for this clusterfuck when the Feds ride in."

"Feds?" She turned her narrowed eyes on me again. "What do you mean, Feds?"

I could hear the frenetic Main Street nightlife clearly, this single corner was all that stood between us and the idiot exuberance of a drunken Friday night in downtown East Paradise Valley. This side street was empty, at least for now. I had a tough time believing no one had heard the gunfire below. Maybe they had but were having too good a time to clear out. Maybe they were hanging around to enjoy the fireworks.

I found it *impossible* to believe that more of Finke's crew were not up here, co-mingling with the city's psychotic nightlife.

"I have a friend with the local FBI office," I explained, anxious to get this show back on the road. I thought it might be counterproductive, not to mention time wasting, to admit that it had been a few years since we'd actually been *friendly* with each other.

It was complicated.

Her glare continued unabated for a moment, then softened. She nodded.

"You think you can trust this friend, and you know you can't trust the cops. So," she shrugged to concede the point. *What else could you do?*

"Honey."

"Da?" In her moment of stress she seemed to forget which language we were speaking in. It was almost cute.

"Thanks for not leaving me behind." I peeked around and behind; the coast was clear in those directions, and the people wandering past on Main couldn't see Finke on the ground at my feet. My Ventura was hiding him from their view.

God, I love a big muscle car!

"Welcome," she said.

"Now could you get the keys and open the trunk for me. I want to get this trash," I gave Finke a none-too-gentle tap on the backside with my own much more appropriate shoe, "loaded up so we can scram."

"Keep litter in its place," she said, and I pictured a sexy cartoon Natasha Fatale in a television PSA.

But she didn't move right away.

"Why are you helping me?"

"Because helping you will probably help me. We're in the same mess." I gave her what I hoped was a winning smile, "I'm also a pretty nice guy."

She returned my forged smile with a raised eyebrow, as if to say *nice guy . . . we both know better than that*. But she went to get the keys.

"I bet Trouble was happy to see you again."

She favored me with another of her patented *what the hell are you talking about* looks, and popped the trunk.

"Your macaw," I explained, and after a moment she actually smiled.

"His name is Mr. Blue," she said. She tilted her head a bit regarded me with some humor, "But Trouble fits him well enough."

I lifted Finke from the ground, I was already tired of having to support the dickhead's boneless bulk, and tumbled Finke into the Ventura's trunk. It was nowhere near as roomy as the Lincoln's and nowhere near as empty. He would have a spare tire, a jack, and a toolbox for company. I plotted my route back to the office. Not necessarily the quickest route either. I planned to hit every pothole and badly patched stretch of pavement I could on the way back to the office.

Payback was a bitch.

I bound his hands behind his back with a roll of speaker wire, then his ankles. If the fucker woke up now he wouldn't be able to pull any tricks when I unlocked the trunk. I actually kind of wanted him to wake up.

Honey moved Mr. Blue's cage to the backseat and belted it in, then slid into the passenger seat. The bird let out a brief squawk of irritation, then quieted. I slid behind the wheel with great relief, made a quick U-turn and left downtown behind. Once we reached the office we could plan our next move. Whatever it turned out to be, I hoped it would be a good one.

CHAPTER 22

Mr. Blue slept while we drove, following the river that separated the East and West Valley until the city's lights were far behind us. A sharp turn took us southeast on Tammany Creek Road, a detour around the city instead of through it. It was the long way back for sure, surrounded by countryside from which a series of sprawling farms, ranches, and horse stables sprouted like weeds along the quiet two-lane road. The speed limit jumped to 45 miles per hour, not that I was bothering with speed limits. I called this the Shit-kicker District, and it cradled East Paradise Valley like a cupped palm for ten miles before hooking north again and climbing a short hill into The Height's affluent residential district.

We weren't going that far. Sixth Street dropped down from the Heights at the seven-mile mark. A left on Sixth, then another left where Airport Road intersected would put us on another short half loop past a gun range, a land-fill, a golf course, and then the airport itself. We would come to my office before reaching the airport. Airport

Road was the worst road in or around town, the constantly sinking ground making cracks, pits, and wild humps in the pavement. I planned to hit them all as hard as possible. I was going to make the last few miles of Finke's ride an adventure; when it was over he was going to feel like an old pair of undershorts in a bad-tempered clothes dryer.

Once again I'd almost forgotten about the fucking bird until he started bitching again, about my driving no doubt.

We were passing the rock quarry, the last real business before the Shit-kicker District, when Mr. Blue came awake screeching.

It was a sound like alarms, air raid sirens, the blasting of apocalyptic trumpets. Fucking loud. I damn near drove us off the road.

I screamed in response, startled at first, then angry.

Honey's startled shout dissolved into laughter, wild, out of breath laughter, and she turned to retrieve the cage.

"How's my good boy doing? How's my Blue Boy?"

"Here comes trouble," the bird replied, and I found the urge to check my rearview mirror irresistible.

No trouble behind us. Not yet anyway. The only trouble present was there in the car with me, and I had a feeling that where trouble was concerned, the bird had nothing on his mistress.

"So," Honey said, returning her attention to me. "Where are we going and what will we do next?"

"My office. It's safe," I assured her, intercepting and interpreting a look of uncertainty. "Then we wait until morning. If we don't hear back from . . . my friend, or my uncle, then we can start reaching out again."

"Why don't we just call Candy's father?" Honey asked. She'd opened the cage door and began stroking Mr. Blue's feathered neck.

He seemed to be enjoying it immensely.

"Happy, happy . . . joy, joy."

"What possible good could that do?" A billboard-sized sign for Lucky's Ranch slipped by on our left, then Five Mile Lane on our right. "He won't know the straight cops from the crooked ones."

"He probably has a better idea than you do," she said, and Mr. Blue ruffled as if catching some of her irritation by telepathy. Her voice was low, conversational, her tone level, but I was sure as shit sensing the tension.

Mr. Blue renewed his profane discourse, and she soothed him to silence.

I waited for her to explain, but she didn't feel the necessity. I was obviously missing something.

"Okay, Honey, you're going to have to fill me in on what I'm missing here."

She turned and watched me for what seemed a very long moment, her gaze at first skeptical, then considering.

I saw Sixth Street ahead, slowed, and turned left onto it. Almost home now.

"Your good guy act was cute, at first, but I'm in no mood to have my intelligence insulted." She fixed me with her dark gaze, pinned me with it like a bug on corkboard. "There are no knights in shining armor."

"Chivalry is dead."

"Da . . . yes," she corrected herself. "And even if it weren't, you just don't look the type."

I said nothing as the Airport Road junction drew

closer, just waited for her to start making sense. I hoped she'd get around to it soon.

"What were you to him? A mule? A dealer? Just another of his strong men?" She faced forward again, giving her head a little shake, as if to dismiss the questions. "It doesn't matter. You did something to piss him off and now you're trying to save yourself. For all I know you're the one who gave Candy her last needle, but if you know Cameron Finke then you know why Candy was his favorite party girl."

"Honey, I'm just the fucking repo man. Finke wants me dead because I found a corpse in the trunk of his Mustang."

Honey pinned me with that bug on a corkboard look again, but it didn't last long. After making my left on Airport Road I turned to her again and found a mirthless smile on her face.

"Just a *repo man,*" she repeated, then laughed, a laugh as humorless as her grin. "You must have the world's worst luck."

"You don't know the half of it," I said. "Wanna tell me what I'm missing?"

She sighed. "Candice Reynolds is your stereotypical good girl gone bad. Good family, nice home, lots of money, an overblown sense of entitlement. Not to speak ill of the dead, or about a friend, but Candy was a spoiled rotten bitch. To keep the story short, she left home with a lot of bad feelings, convinced that her mother and father were the cause of all her problems, determined to prove that she could make it without their help."

Mildly interesting I thought, but not at all helpful. If

this abbreviated biography had a punch line, I hoped she would get to it soon.

"There was nothing noble about her determination. She was just a willful spoiled child, and when she discovered she couldn't maintain the standard of living she was used to with poor boyfriends and minimum wage jobs she found other ways to . . . supplement her income."

How coy, I thought.

Headlights flashed into my rearview mirror from Sixth Street's junction with Airport Road. I saw them and dismissed them in the same second. If Finke's boys back in town had caught our trail, they would have been on it long before.

I was simply too tired to maintain the proper level of paranoia. It had been a long night.

"Finke was fond of Candy because sticking it in her was his way of sticking it to *The Man*." She shrugged, a rueful gesture. "As far as I could tell he was right."

"Okay, so who's *The Man*?"

"Her father, John Reynolds. Paradise Valley's District Attorney."

"Fuck me," I muttered.

John Reynolds, Esquire; a not-so-pleasant blast from my not-too-distant past. The tight-ass DA who'd built a convincing circumstantial case against me five years before. The man who had tried, twice, to throw me in prison. He'd never actually apologized for the above-and-beyond attention he'd shown me because it was not personal to him. It was a high-profile case in an election year, and I was a convincing villain. At least he had the good grace to back down when the killing started again and I had the best of alibis, a nice holding cell in the county jail, awaiting trial.

I kind of figured he owed me one.

"Sorry big boy, but there will be no fucking tonight," Honey said, "I'm off duty and you're not my type."

Smart ass.

I passed my borrowed cell phone to her and said, "Call *The Man.*"

My regrettable lack of paranoia came back and bit me on the ass before she got the chance. The headlights that had only been distant twinkles a few moments before were now blinding and immediate, and the flash of blue and red told me my situation was about to get a lot worse.

"Pull over," Honey said.

"Not a chance."

"Butch," she said, continuing in the slow and patronizing tones one might use when trying to explain to a slow child that pissing on an electric fence was a bad idea. "There is no way this heap is going to outrun a Police Interceptor."

"*Wadaya mean heap?*"

"I'm sorry, *classic.*"

"*Heap-a-shit,*" Mr. Blue squawked, and with real feeling.

"No!"

The cop gave us a brief blat from the siren. Very brief.

"You were speeding," Honey said in her *don't piss on the electric fence* voice. "This one might be legit."

"And if he's not," I said, but was already slowing. There was a wide spot in the road ahead, the turnoff to the long-abandoned shooting range. Only in a city like this would someone build a shooting range a mile away from an airport. People had protested the weird location for years, it was a constant topic of debate at city council, and the terrorist scare that began in September of 2001 finally compelled the city to shut it down.

"He will do one of two things," Honey said, reigning in her tone now that I appeared to be seeing reason. "He'll either ask you for your license and registration or pull his gun and try to kill us."

"That's comforting," I said.

"I said *try*," Honey reminded me.

Her hand crept down her leg and began to pull the silky black cloth of her dress up, revealing her thighs, inch by inch. For a moment I forgot to watch the road and I had to come down a little harder on the brakes than Mr. Blue was happy with to stop before nailing the shooting range fence. I remembered the holster strapped to the happy spot high up beneath her dress and reminded myself that there was slightly more pressing business than getting a peek at her goodies.

Maybe later if I was lucky.

Ah hell, who was I kidding? She'd already said I'm not her type.

CHAPTER 23

The cop pulled in behind me, parked, and for a minute did nothing. Running my plates to see who I was, checking for outstanding tickets, warrants, whether or not I was an axe murderer. Following procedure instead of rushing in with weapon drawn. Very promising.

I put my hands on the wheel and waited like a good boy.

"What is he waiting for?" Honey seemed impatient to proceed. So was I. If this was one of the good ones, he might help.

A few more minutes passed and nothing continued to happen. My hope melted away and a familiar dread took up its accustomed place in my heart.

"Waiting for backup," Honey said.

I wished like hell she hadn't.

"Go! Go now!" She reached for my ignition keys and I blocked her hand.

"Too late for that," I said, staring into the rearview

mirror. Another set of headlights was approaching quickly. Very quickly.

No lights, no siren, tires squealing as the car attached to those headlights slid past us and parked at a slant, blocking us in.

The cop that jumped out of the second car was not following procedure. He crouched behind the trunk of his cruiser, gun drawn, shouting.

"Get out and put your fucking hands in the air!"

"What now?" Honey asked.

I watched the gun for a second, then the face set above it. It was a face that meant business.

"I say we get out and put our fucking hands up . . . but be ready."

"Yes," Honey said. "Always."

We pushed the doors open, put our fucking hands up, got out.

"Step away from your vehicle sir . . . approach my car and put your hands on the trunk!"

I did it, slowly, glad to have his eyes on me. He couldn't watch us both.

"Kelly, what the hell are you doing?" A woman's voice and swift footfalls from my blindside.

I moved toward the cop's cruiser as slowly as possible, and when he finally turned his attention away from me, toward the approaching woman, I stopped. I felt like I'd taken on a bit too much this time and was happy to let cop number one take over for a bit. I shot a quick glance toward Honey and found her on the safe side, relatively speaking, of the Ventura, her hands still raised.

"You said you needed to question them." The lady cop

gave me a wide berth, keeping her eyes on me as she passed. She hadn't drawn her gun, but her right hand rested on the butt. "If I'm missing something then *please* fill me in."

"Logan, these two are dangerous. We found Everett's ride over by Redwolf Bridge earlier tonight but not Everett. I have reason to believe these two may have had something to do with it."

Officer Logan regarded me again, then Honey, but didn't draw her gun.

I smiled hopefully, gave a friendly little wave. "Is it all right if I say . . ."

"*Shut your suck-hole,*" Officer Friendly screamed. "Hands on the fucking trunk!"

Then he pointed his gun at Honey.

"*You too, cunt!*"

"*Stand down Kelly,*" Logan shouted, real alarm in her voice. "*You're out of line!*"

Officer Kelly regarded Logan again. The second his eyes left me I stopped. Honey stopped too, then actually took a step back toward the Ventura's open door.

"Logan, you have no idea what you're doing," Officer Friendly said. "Thanks for your assistance, but you need to get back in your car and drive away."

Logan stood for a moment, silent, her face registering only shock.

"You're out of line," she repeated then turned her back on him and stalked back toward her car. "I'm calling this in."

Bad idea.

"*Look out,*" Honey screamed.

Logan started to turn again, but only in time to see

Officer Friendly's gun pointing at her, not near enough time for evasive action.

He fired and the slug lifted her from her feet.

She hit the ground gasping, clawing first at her chest, then for her holstered gun.

A new noise joined the fray, a muted screaming and the sound of a certain dirtbag's head slamming against the inside of the Ventura's trunk.

"I told you to stay out of it," Officer Friendly said, advancing on her. He sounded almost regretful. "Why do rookies always have to question authority?"

He took aim again, at her head this time no doubt.

I went for the Beretta in my pocket, but Honey was quicker.

She fired, her bullet taking him in the stomach. He doubled over and hit the ground squirming. The gun skittered from his hand, spun across the blacktop and into the ditch on the other side.

Amazingly, he wriggled across the street after it.

Then I remembered the Kevlar vest that had saved me from Finke's cop-killer at the beginning of that crazy night. And if Kelly were still alive . . .

I shoved the gun back in my pocket, I didn't want to have to explain why I had a police issue Beretta in my hand while I was trying to save her. It would only complicate things.

"Get back in the car," I shouted at Honey as I crouched down over Logan.

Logan gave me a look of pure alarm, but didn't fight me when I grabbed her under the armpits and dragged her out of the road.

"Help me up," she said. She was hoarse, out of breath.

Getting shot in the chest will do that to you every time, even if you are wearing a bulletproof vest.

I helped her to her feet, keeping a nervous eye on Officer Friendly. He was shaking off the iron punch to his stomach, had progressed from wriggling to crawling in a matter of seconds.

Logan stood on her own, then leaned against the front of her car. She pushed me away and finally managed to draw her gun.

"Stop, Kelly!" She still wasn't up to shouting, but got out a pretty commanding bark. "Stop or I'll shoot!"

Kelly made it to the ditch, but not his gun. He raised his eyes to her. His face had bad loser written all over it. He stayed on his knees but raised his hands.

"Use my radio," she said. "Call it in . . . please."

She coughed and there was blood on her lips.

Her vest had stopped the slug, but she had a broken rib, maybe more than one, and a punctured lung.

"Hurry," she whispered. "I feel like I'm drowning."

I passed in front of her as quickly as I could, even if her gun was a friendly one I didn't like its unfriendly end pointing at me, and slipped inside the open door.

I wasn't quick enough.

As I was bent down, fumbling for her radio handset, I heard a groan, the squelching sound of flesh pressed against glass, and looked up to see her free hand sliding down the glass, fighting for a hold that wasn't there. There was a thump as she hit the ground, and the gunfire began again.

I dove forward onto the seat, and a moment later broken glass and slugs peppered the air where my head had been. Logan cried out one last time, and the sound was cut off with a mortal swiftness.

Honey returned fire, sending a shot every few seconds. It was covering fire, my opportunity to get the fuck out. I decided to make the most of it, pushed the police cruiser's passenger door open and dove from the cab.

Honey was now sitting behind the wheel so I ran to the Ventura's open passenger door.

She fired it up while I was still moving and threw it into drive as I slid in beside her. We were moving before I got the door shut, but not back on the road. Logan's car blocked us from the back, Officer Friendly's on the front and side. She spun the wheel hard to the right and gunned it down the gravel road into the closed down firing range, and when we reached the locked gate at the end she closed her eyes and pressed down even harder on the gas.

I cringed.

In a fight between an old '70s Pontiac Ventura and a woven-wire gate, the Ventura will usually win, but it doesn't drive away without a few new scars.

"You should know this is the only way in or out," I said.

"I was afraid you were going to say that," Honey said. "And you're welcome."

CHAPTER 24

Funny story—true story. I figured you could use a bit of comic relief about now, before shit gets serious again.

It was my sophomore year in high school, fall, Driver's Education. Our group hit the road about a half-hour after school ended and went until around six in the evening. There were four in my group, Mr. Newmier's group, and the three hours or so we spent in the crappy old Plymouth K Car every evening was joyless. Newmier didn't believe that cars and fun should mix. He was a grumpy old fuck who taught Earth Science during the day and Driver's Education in the evening, a career choice most of us kids wondered about because he obviously hated kids. Bad kids, nice kids, noisy kids, quiet kids. He treated them all with equal contempt.

Marcy, I don't remember her last name, was a quiet, mousy, bespectacled thing who seemed to fear everything and everyone in the world, and after the first few days of Driver's Education, Mr. Newmier was at the top of her *To-Be-Feared* list.

Unfortunately for the rest of us, her fear usually manifested itself in a complete inability to operate a motor vehicle.

Our route led us from school through the residential district, into downtown East Paradise Valley, across the bridge into the West Valley, then on the highway west out of town for about ten miles. Then back again. We did the route twice before landing back at school.

The order in which we drove changed daily. One day I'd get to cruise the relatively calm four o'clock pre-rush streets of residential and East Valley downtown, the next, I might be cruising back through the East Valley when all hell broke loose on the streets at just after five and everyone wanted to be home *now*. The worst driving shift was the second loop heading out of town, and we all dreaded the day when Marcy What's-Her-Name landed behind the wheel for her turn through that homicidal after work free-for-all.

When it finally happened, it was worse than we could have imagined.

"The speed limit is fifty-five," Mr. Newmier said, and began thumping the worn foam of the dash with the palm of his right hand, his signal to speed the fuck up. The left hand he kept ready at all times to seize the steering wheel should the need arise, which it often did with Marcy.

I sat behind the grouchy old fart on that day and had a good view of Marcy's pinched and blushing face.

She was driving no faster than forty-five, and the traffic was stacking up behind us like a high speed game of dominoes.

The boy sitting directly behind her was holding tight to his *Oh Shit* handle, and the girl sitting between us had a hand hovering over each of our legs, fingers bent into claws, ready sink them in if she needed something to hold on to.

Newmier's rhythmic *tap-tap-tapping* sped up, and I grabbed my *Oh Shit* handle to keep my hand occupied. It wanted to reach out and swat the back of his head.

"Speed up! Speed up!"

She sped up, all the way to fifty. She watched the speedometer with grim determination, and Newmier grabbed the steering wheel to negotiate a corner she completely failed to notice, saving us all from a trip through the guardrail and into the river.

Marcy squealed with fright, blushed harder, focused back on the road, dropped back to forty.

Newmier's *tap-tap-tap* became *whap-whap-whap*.

"Fifty-five," he all but bellowed at her. "Speed up!"

The man behind us, no more than an inch or two from our bumper, began *beeping* his horn almost in time with Newmier's whapping.

I turned to have a look.

His face was glowing red with rage. He leaned over his steering wheel, his teeth bared.

Beep-beep-beep . . .

Whap-whap-whap . . .

I faced forward again and saw tears leaking from Marcy's eyes.

"*Speed up!*"

Beep-beep-beep . . .

Whap-whap-whap . . .

I saw an amazing thing, Marcy moving past fear and somewhere into anger in no more than a blink.

She stomped down on the gas and we lurched

forward, or came as close to a lurch as a K Car can manage anyway.

I leaned forward for a better look at the speedometer.

We were now going sixty.

The guy behind us continued to hug our bumper, but at least let off the horn.

"Fifty-five," Newmier bellowed, and tapped the instructor's brake on his side of the car.

The asshole behind us smacked into our rear bumper and laid down on the horn. Another peek back revealed an impressive display of road rage—red faced, spit flying, fist waving.

"Pull over . . . goddamnit!" Newmier seemed ready to give the guy behind us a run for his money in the rage department

Weeping openly, Marcy slowed and pulled into the breakdown lane.

More horns honked and cars swerved out of the way as the asshole behind us leapt from his car and ran toward us.

Marcy's mouth dropped open and froze when she saw him running toward her.

Newmier jumped out of the K Car's passenger door and shuffled around the front of the Driver's Ed car to head him off.

I saw where it was going, made a call, probably a bad one, and opened my door.

Newmier and Asshole were nose to nose on the white line, traffic swerving dangerously around them. Neither of them noticed me as I waved Marcy into the passenger seat and climbed in behind the wheel.

The call might have been bad but the timing was good.

Asshole picked Newmier up and gently heaved him aside, then dove for the door just as I pulled it closed.

"Fucked up my car!" He punched the window, shattered it, and reached for me.

I put my foot down on the gas and damn near took his hand off as I merged back into traffic.

"We are so fucked," a small voice said from the backseat.

I didn't say anything. No need to repeat the obvious.

A few seconds later I saw the asshole's car speeding along the breakdown lane, trying to catch up. Doing a good job of it too. As a getaway car the Plymouth K left a lot to be desired. We topped out at sixty-five, then stayed there as the asshole's car pulled even with us in the breakdown lane.

I looked at him.

He looked at me and grinned.

I knew what he was about to do and there was nothing I could do to stop him.

"Fifty-five," Marcy squeaked from the passenger seat, and stomped down on the instructor's brake.

We juddered and slid to a stop, the cars behind us laying on their brakes and their horns in a symphony of angry rush hour chaos. The asshole who had been beside us only a second before made his move.

He'd meant to ram us, but instead passed in front of us at sixty-five, crossed the oncoming lane, slipping neatly through a gap in the oncoming traffic completely untouched, and shot into the ditch.

I pulled over at the next rest area to vomit and wait for the cops.

We all got off lucky. Mr. Newmier suffered a cracked

rib, the asshole a concussion, broken wrist, assorted cuts and contusions, Marcy a minor nervous breakdown, and I lost a perfectly good lunch, but there was no actual loss of life.

The responding officer didn't shoot or arrest me, but they didn't compliment me on my driving either.

I failed Driver's Ed that time around, but it could have gone worse.

CHAPTER 25

Officer Friendly was after us seconds after we cleared the smashed gate, no siren or flashing lights, and I was pretty sure no pretense at *bringing us in* this time. There were no witnesses left to protest his blatantly unprofessional behavior or remind him of our civil rights. Also, Honey had shot him, and I think he was pretty pissed off about that.

The old range was now just a field overgrown with weeds, one end lined with leaning wooden booths and the other with the weathered remains of ancient target backdrops. The largest structure stood between the gravel parking lot and shooting field, a simple, small clubhouse where members paid dues and met to compare caliber sizes.

Local kids used the place as a handy and out of the way party place. The walls were covered with graffiti, the parking lot littered with trash. A large ring of scorched rocks in the center of the field contained the remains of long dead bonfires. I'd been there twice before, once to round up a bail-jumper for Uncle Higheagle, once to rescue the rebellious teenage daughter of an old friend.

She did not thank me for the considerable time and effort I put in to tracking her down, but that's another story for another day.

I don't know what Honey had planned, probably nothing much beyond the immediate problem of putting a little distance between herself and the hereafter, but I couldn't argue with her priorities.

The Ventura was a good car, solid, straight and fast, but it was no match for the Interceptor in Officer Friendly's cruiser, and he was on our ass in no time. He drew up close behind us in the parking lot, drifted to the right, surged forward, thumping my rear quarter panel in a nicely executed PIT maneuver.

I had no *Oh Shit* handles, so I gripped the dash and held on.

We slid sideways, would have flipped over if we'd been on blacktop, but the gravel was a more forgiving surface. We spun though, round and round, the badly lit landscape around us blurring as it spun around us. I closed my eyes, I may even have screamed a bit.

Honey didn't make a sound.

When the spinning stopped I opened my eyes and found the countryside rushing past again. Honey was back in full control and glaring through the windshield.

"Shut up you big baby."

I could think of no clever response to that. I was beyond clever responses, or even coherent ones. I bit my lips and hoped I'd be around to think of a good one later.

Officer Friendly had fallen behind again, but was closing the gap.

"Hold on!" Honey turned sharply where the gravel lot ended and gave way to a rocky slope, the kind of natural ramp that would have been perfect for a Dukes of Hazard stunt jump, but usually only ended in blood and tears in the real world. We slid again, then shot out into the open field of the firing range. I saw Honey grin at the rearview mirror, but the grin faded when Officer Friendly made the same turn, completely failing to fall for her trap. He even gained a few more yards on us.

She put her foot down harder on the gas and the Ventura bounced and skittered across the rough and rocky ground, shaking me from seat to ceiling like a ball in a pinball machine.

"Can't this piece of shit go any faster?"

"Watch it!"

"Sorry, I did not mean to insult your piece of shit!"

She yanked the wheel hard to the left, just avoiding the fire pit in the center of the field.

Officer Friendly avoided it just as easily.

"Shit," Honey said.

I was too busy being her pinball to respond.

She swerved right, left, right, then yanked the steering wheel hard left. We made a rough, bouncing U-turn that threw me face-first into the passenger side glass and side-swiped two of the old leaning booths. Wood flew in splinters and Honey demonstrated her mastery of the English language in a blue streak that would have made a West Valley crack whore blush.

Officer Friendly stomped on his brakes, missed the booths, but fell behind again.

"Hey!" Honey kept her eyes on the road, or lack of road in front of us, but slapped my arm when I didn't respond.

"*What?*"

Honey stomped the gas again but kept the Ventura straight, aiming for the parking lot. Officer Friendly wasted no time catching up to us. He was closing in on us fast.

"*Do cop cars have airbags?*" I heard her scream clearly enough, but my shaking brain was about as useful to me as a Jell-O fruit salad. It took a few seconds to put her words in context.

"What . . . no, don't!"

She did.

Officer Friendly was closing in again, setting us up for another PIT maneuver, and Honey stomped on the brakes.

We did that sliding thing that I love so much. I saw Officer Friendly's *Holy Shit* face over the hood of his ride and moving fast toward the Ventura's rear passenger door as he responded by stomping down on his brakes.

Too little too late, as they say. He clobbered the same rear panel he'd already dented, pushed my side of the car clean off the ground, and I was looking at sky as we flipped over and started to roll.

<hr>

When I opened my eyes the world seemed reluctant to come back into focus. Behind me, Mr. Blue flapped and squawked indignantly from inside his cage, but it was still belted in and he seemed to be okay. Finke flopped around inside the trunk, clearly displeased with the seating arrangement, but clearly still alive. The driver's seat was empty, the side window busted out, so Honey had managed to free herself.

All the bells of hell were ringing inside my bruised and battered brain-cage, so I was clearly still alive as well.

I should have been grateful, but gratitude had settled somewhere near the bottom of my current emotional stew.

No way I was letting Honey drive again.

Gunfire startled me from my ungenerous, drifting thoughts, and I fumbled for my seatbelt. I didn't even remember buckling up. I'd probably done it without thinking after Honey's assault on the gate.

Another shot, a scream from Honey. Frustration instead of pain.

My passenger door was uncooperative but popped open when I put my shoulder to it. The poor abused Ventura had landed right side up but now looked like I felt.

The cruiser was a few yards away, the radiator sending out stinking plumes of steam and the deflating airbags filling up the cab. The driver's door stood open.

I saw Officer Friendly a moment later, gun drawn and pointing his way as he approached one of the old booths. I could see Honey crouching low inside it, clutching her gun but not firing.

I felt inside my jacket, found a gun, flicked off the safety as I drew, aimed, fired. He was fifty feet away, give or take, and I wasn't that good of a shot. I didn't think I'd hit him, but distract him away from Honey, sure.

The gun flew from his hand, discharged as it hit the ground.

He clutched his arm, screamed, ululating and high-pitched, then fainted.

My first few steps in his direction were unsteady, the gongs were sounding loud and clear inside my head again, but the world had more or less stopped trying to tip me off by the time I reached him.

He was still clutching his arm and blood flowed freely from between his fingers.

"You should have shot that pig in his head," Honey said, almost growled from behind me. She walked with a limp, but I thought she was lucky to be walking at all. She regarded the Glock in her hand, glared at it actually, and deftly slipped it back into her thigh holster. The action momentarily revealed most of her thighs, and there was a stir of interest from Little Butch again.

I wished she'd quit doing that. It was distracting.

"Out of bullets," she said, then directed her glare at me as if she'd just read my thoughts. Probably she had.

"I was aiming for his head," I said, trying to direct her annoyance away from me. I nudged Officer Friendly with the toe of my boot. He rolled with it, his hand losing its loose grip on the injured arm. The hole in it was large and still leaking blood, but it looked like the slug had gone all the way through, and the wound was starting to clot. He'd probably live until morning. I gave him a gentle kick to express my mixed feeling about that. It made me feel a little better.

"And you're welcome," I said to Honey.

She wanted to cap him where he lay, but with the proper application of reason I persuaded her to spare his life.

"Give me your gun!"

"No."

She made a visible effort to calm herself and attempted to deconstruct my reason for refusing her perfectly reasonable request. "I only want to shoot him a little."

"No." I had other plans for him.

"He called me a *cunt*!"

I ignored her and unclipped the handcuffs from his belt.

"Help me drag him."

"No," she said, and stalked away with her arms crossed. *Oh well.*

I stripped him of his belt and holster, found his handcuff keys and tossed them into the weed-choked field, dragged him toward the fence. I cuffed him and left him there, content in the knowledge that come morning he might get a chance to see how the other half lived. I hear ex-cops are very popular in prison.

Honey passed us, walking back toward the road with Mr. Blue's cage in her arms.

"Where are you going?"

She ignored me, kept walking.

My head hurt too much to argue. I walked back to the Ventura and considered it for a moment.

A Pontiac Ventura is a tough car, but roll one once or twice and it's going to show. The hood was partially caved in, the side panels and doors smashed almost flat, the rear bumper twisted. She was going to need more than a wax and a buff to make her pretty again.

The lights were still on, though a little dimmer than I usually like to see them. They'd been running off the battery for five, maybe ten minutes, but they *did* still work.

The driver's door required some persuasion but I got it open, found the key still slotted in the ignition where Honey had left it and gave it a turn. To my happy surprise, it started right up.

I met Honey by the road and took a moment to enjoy the shock on her face as she watched me roll up to her. Probably not up to her usual standards, but hell, it beat walking.

She shook her head, but smiled and climbed into the passenger seat.

"Well, what are we waiting for?"

"There's something I need to grab," I said, climbing out as she shut her door. I approached Officer Logan's car.

She lay slumped against the front of her cruiser, her ruined head resting against her breasts.

"Sorry," I said, and I was. She had been one of the good ones.

Inside the car her dash cam was still recording. I pushed the stop button and pulled it from its mount. The recording would go a long way toward helping me prove my story, if I lived long enough to tell it to the people that mattered.

It would also make sure Officer Friendly got exactly what he deserved.

Back in the Ventura, once again rolling down the blacktop toward safety, I said, "Didn't you have a call to make?"

CHAPTER 26

I listened to Honey's conversation with John Reynolds Esquire, AKA Candy's daddy, with a sick kind of fascination. I could hear his part of the dialog, not as words, but a staccato squawking. It was more like the *wa-wa-wa* sounds the adults made on those old Charlie Brown cartoons than speech. No words, but his volume . . . well, it spoke volumes. Loud, clipped, curt. What few doubts I had about his resistance to belief were immediately squashed by Honey.

Honey handled him with more tact than I could have managed, even when his voice rose high enough to hurt her ears, she kept her cool with him. Not compassion, but a purely pragmatic empathy. She wanted him to understand, but not fall apart. She wanted him to grieve, but she wanted his grief on our side.

I reckoned that if she ever got tired of turning tricks and giving lap dances for a living, she'd make a fair headshrinker.

But Mr. DA was not buying it. He was angry at being

awakened, angrier that someone would awaken him to pull such a sick and mean joke.

His voice rose a few more decibels, I could hear the words bitch and arrested clearly in a mix of incoherencies, and Honey held the speaker away from her ear, wincing as if she had a sudden headache. Her calm was beginning to break down. I could see anger creeping in to replace it.

I held my hand out for the phone and she passed it over without hesitation, looking relieved to be rid of it.

"He's just as stubborn as she said."

"Mr. Reynolds," I said, raising my voice to match his, but not shouting. "If you think we're fucking with you why haven't you hung up yet?"

Beside me, Honey looked shocked. More than shocked, appalled.

Mr. DA's rant broke off in mid-streak, and I took advantage of his silence.

"Candy has a mark just below her belly button, shaped like a cherry. I thought it was a tattoo for a second but it isn't. Not a mole either, not hairy enough."

A few more seconds of silence, then Mr. DA started again.

"Look, whoever you are, I . . ."

I cut him off.

"I have a picture of her with the macaw at the golf course." I let go of the steering wheel for a second to pat down my breast pocket, wanting to make sure I did still have it. It was still there, along with the IDs I'd lifted from Tattoo and Musclehead. I remembered with a slight shock that those men were both dead now, I'd killed one and Honey the other, and somehow the thought of these laminated cards in my pocket brought a new dimension of reality to the night.

I have really stepped in the shit this time, I thought.

"There's something written on the back," I continued, "but I never got a chance to read it."

Mr. DA did not interrupt, but his end of the line was not silent. His breathing was heavy, hitching.

"Do you know the picture I'm talking about?"

Total silence, held breath, then, "Yeah, I know it."

Another break in the conversation, and this time I held my silence.

"What's written on the back?"

He already believed us, but he needed to hear it, so I let the Ventura drift to the shoulder of the road, the gated entrance to the golf course just ahead. Not the golf course in Candy's picture, which was a members only course for the very rich, this one was a recreation spot for the middle class, less expensive, less accommodating, and always stinking of the landfill it shared a hillside with.

When I'd pulled over and checked that no one was about to come from behind and clobber the old Ventura again, I turned on the dome light and pulled the picture from my breast pocket.

I turned it over, read what was there to read, and for a second was unable to talk. My eyes burned, my throat locked up as if I were choking on the grief that should have been Mr. DA's. In a way I was.

"Team Reynolds's big day. Who needs a trophy when I have you? Thanks for being there with me."

I couldn't finish right away. I had to stop. I had to remember to breathe. Breathing was suddenly very hard to do.

"With love, daddy."

There was a very long pause.

I slipped the picture back into my breast pocket, turned off the dome light, and pulled back onto the road.

"It was the father-daughter tournament," Reynolds said. "We placed fifth. A year later she left."

Then he began to weep.

I couldn't take any more of it. I passed the phone to Honey. "He's all yours."

I ignored the way she looked at me, stared straight ahead as I picked up speed. Only a few more miles to the office.

"Mr. Reynolds, we have the bastard who did it," again her Natasha Fatale accent came shining through, "but he has a lot of friends, and they have been trying very hard to kill us. We don't know who we can trust. We need your help."

Honey did very little talking over the next few minutes, was silent except for the occasional answered question, and as I pulled up to the security gate and rolled my window down to key in my code, she passed the cell phone back to me.

"Yes?"

"Who exactly am I speaking to?"

I wondered if using my real name would fuck up the deal. It was only a few years past that he'd demonstrated a burning desire to see me fry or rot in jail. I decided to go for it. "Quick. Butch Quick."

"Okay, Mr. Quick. We're on the same team for now." He was clearly struggling to keep his emotions under control, and the fact that he seemed to be winning the battle impressed me. I just hoped I wouldn't have to be around when this was over and the floodgates finally opened. "This is going to take a little time but I'm going to make some calls. I'm only going to call the few people I know I can trust, and we'll get the ball rolling."

I felt my stress level fall a few notches. It was a great relief to have someone with a clear idea of where the fuck to start on my side, a greater one to have at least a little bit of this weird burden resting on a set of better qualified shoulders. It was also nice to know he'd apparently gotten past his desire to see me drawn and quartered, then throw the pieces into a prison cell to rot.

"Do you have a safe place?"

I answered in the affirmative, and when he asked where it was, I gave him my location and my pass code.

"One last thing, Mr. Quick."

"Yes sir."

The *sir* came with no forethought. The man on the other end of this troubled line somehow seemed to demand it.

"If you are in any way responsible for my girl's death," he was whispering now, and I could almost see him sitting in his quiet and dark study, casting an eye toward the bedroom where his wife still slept, "I will find out, and when I'm finished with you, you're going to wish that Cameron Finke had killed you."

"I understand."

"You don't understand anything," clear contempt in his voice. "Until you've lost a daughter, you don't understand."

I keyed in my code, waited for the gate to slide open, said nothing. I was speechless.

He'd forgotten them, my girls, had let them slip from

his mind, probably the day he realized he wasn't going to be able to hang anyone for their murders. He was a big and important cog in Paradise Valley's legal machine, but he might as well have been flipping burgers.

I wanted to put my hands around his throat and choke the life out of him just then. I think I could have done it with joy.

"Did you hear me?"

I didn't answer right away. I didn't want him to hear the murder in my voice when I did.

"Yes," I said at last, and I thought I faked calm pretty well.

"Do you believe me?"

I thought about my own daughter again, my baby girl, still very young when I lost her. Forever young.

"Yes," I said.

And of course, I did. Goddamn fucking right I did!

CHAPTER 27

All good things end. That is *the* truth of the human condition. Our lives are straw houses, so carefully built, too easily blown down.

Life goes from good, to bad, to worse.

Put that on a fucking Hallmark card and mail it to yourself, because you may need reminding.

The best thing that ever happened to me ended on a bitter-cold winter morning five years before Cameron Finke and Honey came into my life to seriously fuck up a good comfortable rut.

I asked Elizabeth, Beth, out a week after our surprise reunion on the campus where we went to college. I expected her to say no, because it was me asking, but I thought she'd do it kindly, because *she* was kind. She surprised me by saying yes, and before I'd even finished bumbling out the awkward request.

A year after graduation, me working as an engineer for a local outfit with a lot of nice, fat government contracts and her teaching at the same private school she'd attended after her parents pulled her from the public puberty madhouse where we'd first met, I asked her an even bigger question. Again she answered in the affirmative before I'd gotten all the words untangled from my stupid tongue.

She always seemed to be a step ahead of me, waiting for me to catch up, always ready with the answer before I had the question. In the years since, I sometimes forget the power of my love for her, and how she used it to make me a better man. Tiny little thing that she was, she eclipsed everything that happened before, all the bad stuff. None of it mattered when she was there.

Then our daughter came, Daphne Quick, Beth used to joke that it was the name of a comic book super heroine, and her power over me was much the same, except bigger. She was my entire world.

Sometimes the memory of their power, their enormity and absolute centrality in my personal universe faded into the gray of the angry, everyday humdrum. But it always comes back to me, and it's like having them die all over again.

It was winter, it was cold, and I hadn't slept the night before. Beth and Daphne had spent a week on the Oregon Coast, Christmas with her retired parents in Oceanside, and I had stayed behind. I'd told Beth I couldn't get the time off, but it was a lie. I hadn't even tried. Her parents remembered me from all those years ago, not as the boy who had rescued her from a group of bullies, but as the troublemaker who had gotten her into trouble with them in the first place.

I don't know how they arrived at that conclusion, parents are weird when it comes to their children and maybe they just wanted to believe that bad things could never happen to their Elizabeth, that her purity blinded evil to her, protected her. Who knew? They hated me, always had and always would, and I thought they were a couple of self-satisfied, sanctimonious, worthless, clueless prigs.

I thought it would be better for everyone if I just stayed behind.

I think Beth probably knew I lied to her about getting that time off. Whether or not she agreed with it, she went with it.

The hour of her return passed, then several hours. I called her cell phone and got the voicemail. Her parents called me, yelled at me for her not being there, and I hung up on them. A few more hours passed and *I* called *them*, asked if they'd heard from her, and they hung up on me.

When darkness fell and I was still alone I called the police.

They asked if we'd been having marital problems, if she'd maybe run away. I gritted my teeth and answered all their questions as politely as I could.

Early the next morning they called, and an officer in the field asked me for any identifying features. Something on her body, maybe a c-section scar or distinctive mole.

As it happened she had both.

That was when I knew something was wrong, something that would be wrong forever.

I heard the distant chuff of airbrakes, the single warning blat of a cop's siren.

And I ran to my car, the old Ventura I'd fallen in love with at my Uncle Higheagle's classic car lot and picked up on a generous family discount. I ran every red light and shattered the speed limit, out of the East Valley where we lived and loved in a modest home in a good neighborhood and through the West Valley to Redwolf Bridge.

Redwolf had been in and out of the news for three years by then, local and national. Paradise Valley's very own serial killer. He took women, raped them, then destroyed them and arranged what was left of their used up husks on the long arch of concrete called Wawawai Bicentennial Bridge, more popularly known as Redwolf Bridge these days. He displayed them.

The bridge was blocked at both ends by police cars, so I parked in the road and ran. They tried to stop me but there was no way they could have, short of blowing me away.

I found Beth and Daphne where Redwolf had left them.

The details are in the files, not that I need the files to remember. Every drop of blood, ragged scrap of flesh, every dust mote and sparkle of frost was burned into me forever.

The next couple of days however are still a blur. I oscillated from a near comatose grief to murderous rage, and they'd had to sedate me, stick me in that fabled 5th floor of Saint Joseph's Hospital, the one where they keep the funny backward coats and soft rooms, the place where doctors whose false concern masks their impatience to get through another shift so they can spend some quality time at Quail Ridge hitting golf balls and having drinks with the cream of the Paradise Valley crop.

And when they finally let me out it was only to stick me in another cell, where the dead hooker's daddy would try his damndest to take what little was left of my life away.

Of course you know that didn't happen.

Gina White happened instead.

Gina White was a local representative of the FBI, newly installed on the Redwolf case before I was jailed, and somehow no one had missed her for the few days she was absent following my breakdown.

She turned up later, beaten, tortured, raped, but alive, and with the first and only physical evidence ever to turn up in the Redwolf case.

She had escaped, and easily enough she said, but only after he'd raped her. After she had *allowed* him to rape her, for the DNA evidence she'd brought them in a used condom.

Her evidence set me free and pointed the long arm of the law at Roy Dickie.

Roy Dickie, who also had a taste for classic cars, and who Uncle Higheagle had customer files of, credit checks and the likes.

That was how I found him before the cops, even before the FBI. It was the mention in his files of his part ownership in a family run horse stable in the mountains near the Rattlesnake Summit, just a few miles from the Washington-Oregon border. They stabled and cared for animals that belonged to city slickers who liked to pretend to be cowboys on the weekend. It only took a little research to discover the place had been closed for years, shut down when his parents died, and his sibs showed zero interest in helping him run the place.

I found him there, even found Beth's no-style Chrysler Neon parked in the unused stables along with a half-dozen others, all belonging to Redwolf victims as it turned out.

You know what happened then.

We went for a little ride, what was supposed to be our last ride. It was his last, but not mine. If there was a reason I survived, it presented itself not long after they let me out of Saint Joseph's for the second time.

Another broken body arranged on Redwolf Bridge, an arrangement that the serial killer groupies and buffs called artistic expression; and the killer's calling card, the leather wolf's head mask, soaked in the victim's blood and watching over the scene from the footpath's handrail. This time there was a personal message, short and jolly and to the point. A great big *Ha . . . gotcha!*

Roy Dickie had not been working alone. He was not the brains behind the Redwolf crimes, wasn't even the killer. He was only an assistant, a willing accomplice and rapist. A sick fuck, but not *the* sick fuck.

The real killer was still out there, still is to this day.

If there was a reason I survived it was because I still had someone else to kill, but I don't think reason had anything to do with it. Only dumb, blind luck.

CHAPTER 28

The bay door slipped upward and I pulled into my accustomed spot.

"This is your office?" Honey was almost comic in her incredulity. Any amusement I may have felt was tempered by the realization that apparently even Paradise Valley hookers have higher standards than me.

"Would you like me to take you back to your flat?"

"No, I'm sure it's adequate," she said, her tone suggesting that adequate was a fluid term, which adjusted to meet the circumstances. In other words it was preferable to being shot and thrown in the river, but only barely.

"What's wrong with it?" I clicked the remote on my sun visor again, and the door shuddered downward.

"It's a bit seedy, don't you think?"

An exotic dancer whose flat could have come straight from the pages of *Better Whores and Gardens* had just called my office seedy. My night was now complete.

"They sure as shit won't find us here," I pointed out.

The bay door banged to a stop against the concrete floor.

Honey cast a quick glance around, then back to me, smiling. "Yes. It's adequate."

Deciding that was as close to *Nice Digs* as I was going to get out of her, I let it drop.

Sure as shit won't find us here.

If only I'd known.

It was the phone, the fucking phone I'd taken from good old Sleeping Ugly AKA Phil Shepard.

So Finke was not the most trusting of souls, all the cell phones he provided to his band of goons were GPS traceable through his phone, which he'd dropped during our dustup in the service tunnels under downtown.

I credit my survival up to that point to quick thinking and luck, but luck goes both ways. It only takes a little of the bad kind to ruin a person's night.

I checked on Sleeping Ugly first, wanted to make sure he hadn't puked behind his gag of duct tape and maybe choked to death on it. He wasn't dead, but he was sleeping again. I moved him from his little corner of my office, wheeled him like a piece of ugly furniture into the center of the room.

Honey made herself at home, poured herself a cup of coffee, declared it to be just a step above road-mud but drank it anyway. She seated herself on the old sprung sofa and studied Sleeping Ugly like an entomologist observing some strange and previously undiscovered species of roach.

She raised one eyebrow at him when he finally did awaken, facing her, sitting comfortably, or reasonably so, across from him and sipping road-mud from an old and chipped mug instead of dead and somewhere at the bottom of the river.

He was clearly surprised. He made muffled hooting sounds behind his silver strapping tape gag. He bucked against the furniture dolly, sent it rocking and tilting, and for a moment, it looked like he'd go over on his back. After a few seconds, the dolly decided to stay upright, and he aborted the physical portion of his tantrum.

He grunted in Honey's direction again.

"Articulate as ever," Honey said, then yawned.

I popped my Ventura's trunk open and found Finke, the man of the hour, awake, aware, and furious.

The vision made me smile, I couldn't help it, and that smile acted on Finke's fury like gasoline on fire.

"Motherfucker I'm gonna fucking kill you goddamn cocksucker . . ." I'm pretty sure he called me a Bushnigger at some point, gotta admit I've never heard that one before but it lacked in creativity.

I was more than willing to let Finke wear himself out.

He went on like that for a few minutes, eventually losing all intelligibility in grunting exhaustion. His flopping, screaming tantrum didn't help him break loose, the cords of speaker wire stretched a little maybe, but not enough for him to slip a hand or foot free. He did manage to beat the crap out of himself a little more in the process.

A long cut spilled blood down his forehead, a few

gashes in his scalp also trickled blood, a cut on his chin, a tear along the back of his jeans just above the left knee revealed a deep gash with a grimy halo of grease. He had too many small bruises and cuts to count.

It had been a very bumpy ride for Mr. Finke.

"You're bleeding all over my toolbox," I said, and dragged him out by the collar of his shirt. I jerked him up, perhaps a bit harder than necessary, and added a respectable goose egg to his collection of bumps and cuts when his head struck the underside of the trunk lid. I won't count this as a bad thing though, he was a little more easygoing on his drag from the trunk to the office.

"I would love you forever if you untied him," Honey said, and it took a long moment for me to get the sense of what she was saying. It was a tempting prospect, in more ways than one, but I decided against it.

"I'm sure he'd try something, and I know you'd love an excuse to shoot him, but . . ." I dropped him into the old rolling office chair I normally occupied when actually conducting business in my office, "I'd be just as happy if no one else had to die tonight."

She fixed me with her eyes, cold, sharp, considering. For a few seconds I thought she'd draw and begin shooting anyway, if she had anything more than air in her chamber. Finke first, then Sleeping Ugly, then maybe me for telling her no. Then her glare softened and she smiled. It was not a happy expression, but marginally less threatening than the one that preceded it.

"It's your call, Mr. Quick. I've lived with disappointment my whole life. I suppose I can live with a little more tonight."

"Man, you're going to be sorry you ever fucked with

me." Finke sitting slouched forward in my chair, tousled hair hanging down his battered face, spoke these words with absolute honesty, perfect faith. In his mind there was no other way for this to end but him on top and me dead.

Here, I thought, *is a man too used to having everything his own way.* Maybe a little taste of failure would do him some good, thicken his skin a little, remind him that the world doesn't always play by his rules.

Or maybe it wouldn't.

I didn't give much of a fuck.

"Sit tight, slick." I rolled the furniture dolly with Sleeping Ugly over to him, arranged them back to back, or the back of Finke's head to Sleeping Ugly's ass, and went to work with the strapping tape again.

When I finished, Finke's arms were strapped tightly against his sides, his forehead against the high headrest of my chair, and the only visible portion of his face was the ridiculously heroic looking cleft chin and the slightly skewed beak of his nose. He was hobbled, gagged, and blinded by wrap after wrap of the gray tape.

I hoped Finke would be the last prisoner I'd have to take that night.

I was all out of strapping tape. I was hoping to avoid breaking into my last bottle of Crazy Glue.

I thought Honey and I would be in for a few boring and restless hours of waiting followed by several more boring hours of answering questions and giving statements.

I needn't have worried about being bored.

Less than a minute after making Finke feel at home, Sleeping Ugly's phone rang. It gave no name or photo to go with the unfamiliar number, so I answered with some apprehension.

"Phil's Bathhouse and Jack-O-Rama . . ."

"Don't be a jackass, Mr. Quick." There was no pause or doubt in the man's voice, only exhaustion and anger. I recognized him at once.

"Sorry, Mr. Reynolds."

"Are you and the," now there was a pause as Mr. DA tried to find a way of referring to Honey more politic than *whore*. '. . . and Candice's *friend* safe?"

"Safe and snug," I said, and again repeated that thing I'd already said to Honey, the assumption that Finke's scattered and moronic henchmen would never find me in my out of the way office. "No way they'll track us down here."

I think I mentioned earlier that my assumptions are not to be trusted. I know better than anybody how stupid I can be, but sometimes I forget.

Fuck it, I was tired.

"And Mr. Finke?" He sounded positively ferocious.

"Finke and one of his pals, Phil Shepard. I have a great taped confession from Shepard."

Mr. DA spoke over me, completely ignoring this latest intel. "Don't let them out of your sight. I've got the ball rolling but it'll take some time."

I heard a harried feminine voice in the background, Mrs. DA presumably. Harried, but not hysterical. Concerned, but not grieving. He hadn't told her yet.

I stepped around the room's weird centerpiece, a strange piece of underground art that was one part office chair, one part furniture dolly, two parts asshole. I passed from Sleeping Ugly's morose gaze, and stopped directly in front of Finke's gagged and blindfolded face.

"They aren't going anywhere."

Mr. DA hung up without another word.

"A charming man," I said to Finke, speaking very close to his left ear so he would know I was talking to him. "Cuddly as a porcupine and fluffy as a snake. Seems anxious to meet you."

Finke said something behind his gag. Something that might have been *Eat Shit and Die*, or maybe *please let me up, I'm sitting on my nuts*.

Then the phone rang again.

***

This time there was a name to go with the number, and a photograph dredged up from the cell phone's memory of a narrow, gray woman, past middle age but not yet elderly. Long, narrow nose, narrower eyes, and the thinnest lips I've ever seen on a woman. The picture showed her from her bony shoulders up, but I could almost imagine the rest of the woman; limbs like twigs, knobby knees and elbows, flat chest, and a body as slender as a pole. The phone ID'd her as Miss Lizzie.

I showed the picture to Honey, who only shook her head. "I've never seen her before."

Not a regular part of Finke's crew, she certainly didn't look the part, but if her particulars were programmed into this cell phone then she was tied to the man somehow.

It continued to ring and I realized I was out of thinking time. Simple curiosity won out and I pushed the little green button.

"Phil Shepard's answering service, may I take a message?"

"With whom am I speaking?" Miss Lizzie's voice was dusty, but disarming. Not the sharp and miserly thing I'd expected, but curious, friendly. It was a grandma voice.

"Hackman," I answered, giving my old standard alias, one I've used a half-dozen times over the past five years. "Rondo Hackman."

"Well hello, Mr. Hackman." She was positively bubbling over with good humor. "May I ask what kind of trouble my young nephew Cameron is in this time?"

Her nephew, I thought. *Fucking peachy.*

I needed another complication about as much as I needed anal leakage and painful urination.

"What kind of trouble does he usually get in?" Answering questions with questions is a great way to stall for time, though it has an unfortunate side effect of pissing the questioner off. Not that I was concerned about Miss Lizzie. She seemed as hard as milkweed fluff, sharp as dust bunnies.

"Cut the shit, sonny," she said. She did not fall into the strident tones of aged offense. Her voice was as bright, light, and playful as before. "Don't mistake politeness for diffidence. I'm only trying to decide if I want to bother bailing him out this time."

So, the old rip meant business. I decided there wasn't

going to be much gain in continuing the conversation, so I determined to end it quickly.

"I wouldn't worry about it too much. I don't think there will be any bailing him out this time."

I held the phone away from my ear and searched for the end button, but wasn't quick enough to avoid Miss Lizzie's final word on the subject.

A tinkling little laugh, almost pixyish, then, "Don't count on it, Rondo."

***

"Who was that?" Honey sat with Mr. Blue's cage beside her on the couch. The bird cooed and spread its wings to the confines of its cage as she stroked its bib of fine yellow feathers.

"His aunt," I hooked a thumb at Finke, who began to grunt and chuff behind his gag.

Honey jerked forward on the couch, pulling her hand from the open door of Mr. Blue's cage to seek out her gun. She pulled it, remembered it was empty, tossed it aside with a muttered word. Russian I think, it didn't sound like a happy one.

Mr. Blue squawked in irritation, then hopped from his low perch through the cage's open door and crouched on Honey's lap.

"For fuck's sake," I said, finally at my wit's end. "For the last God-damned time, there is no way they're going to find us here!"

She glared at me and resumed stroking Mr. Blue.

"Here," I said, pulled one of Finke's guns from inside my jacket and tossed it to her. "Do you feel better now?"

She hefted it, considering the weapon with the same expression she'd given my office on our arrival, thumbed the safety off.

"Marginally," she said. "And thank you."

"Here comes trouble," Mr. Blue shrieked, taking brief flight before settling back down on his mistress's lap. His wings were tensed, spread, fluttering in anticipation. He faced the small man-sized door at the far end of the room.

Honey adjusted her gaze to the same door, and I followed suit just in time to see it smash open and a half-dozen of Finke's scumbags pour through it like puke through the mouth of a drunk.

CHAPTER 29

They spread and broke apart into two groups of three, flanking the door as yet two more tried to push through simultaneously, jamming shoulder to shoulder in the too narrow opening. They set eyes on Honey, following Mr. Blue's screeching expletives, then they turned to me and began to fire.

I shoved my right hand inside my coat pocket trying to pull iron, but failing miserably, the fucking butt kept catching on the pocket flap and slipped out of my hand entirely. That's when I decided to dive to the floor, now, and worry about my landing later. The landing hurt like hell, but the lunge was well timed. Out of the six shots fired my way, only two hit me.

The first blazed a red line of fire and blood across my back before shattering the coffee pot. The second pierced the lobe of my left ear and grooved the back of my neck.

Then I hit the concrete floor of my office, striking my chin hard enough to break a tooth. A bright starburst, not just stars but a starburst, exploded across my vision before burning out to a muddy, slow darkness.

I heard screaming, laughter, the outraged squawks of Mr. Blue. These things registered with a slow, foggy lack of clarity that I recognized from my deepest drunks, and I realized with something like alarm, or as close to alarm as I could manage in that state, that my lights were going out, were halfway there in point of fact.

I told myself that I must not black out, that if I didn't get my shit in gear at roughly the speed of light Honey would be dead, but that didn't help. I told myself that once Honey was dead they would finish me in very short order, and that the fuckwad Finke would get away, and was unable to bring the world around me back into focus.

I heard Mr. Blue's distant, distorted, and querulous squawking again— *My ass your face, awk!*—and understood that once Honey and I were history they would probably shoot the bird just to make a complete job of it, and strangely, that did the trick.

The fog of sound and blurred sensation arranged itself into pain, fiery and wet across my back, through my mangled ear, the back of my neck, and my face. I'd landed right on my nose, broken it. It dumped blood down my lips and chin, pooled beneath me on the concrete, ruined one of my favorite shirts.

Next came the unique thunder of weapons firing and the burnt rubber stench, strong enough to penetrate even my smashed schnoz, of cheap lacquer-sealed ammunition. Hot-loaded 9mm rounds, cheap shit most likely sold on the black market and originating from somewhere in Eastern Europe.

The scumbag's ammunition of choice.

There was screaming . . .

"Oh shit oh fuck oh shit . . ."

"My head, oh my fuckin' 'ead!"

"Fuck the Seahawks! Awk!"

Mostly there are screams of pain. Men in pain, I realize, and start to feel some fleeting hope.

"No you moron, you'll shoot Cameron!"

This last from a woman, but not Honey. The voice is older, and I didn't recognize it right away because the polite, jolly tone is gone. It was the voice, dusty, angry, clipped, that I expected to go with the narrow and humorless face on Sleeping Ugly's cell phone caller ID.

Miss Lizzie was on the scene, and she was not amused.

But what about Honey?

At last, after what seemed minutes of struggle but was probably only a few seconds, I opened my eyes.

The first thing I saw was the rear wheel of the Ventura; dirty, scuffed, almost out of tread. Then my eyes focused on something closer, something between my face and the tire. It was the gun I'd tried to free from my pocket before taking my dive, not the Beretta, but another of Finke's. Cheap piece of shit or not I was happy to see it.

Apparently unnoticed, maybe they thought I was already dead, I groped for the gun, grasped it, and rolled onto my side to see what all the noise was about.

Four of Finke's men were on the floor in front of the door bleeding from gunshot wounds, three still moving, and one not. This gentleman lay splayed like a ham actor playing dead, arms and legs spread, a huge blooming red patch over his chest. Ham actor pose or not, I didn't think this guy was pretending. Another man stood just over the threshold, his gun pointed at Honey, a look of painful indecision on his pocked and pitted junkie face.

When I turned to look for Honey, the source of his frustration became clear.

Honey was crouched behind the living mixed media sculpture that was half man, half office furniture. Sleeping Ugly, standing tall above Honey and Finke on his furniture cart, was already dead. Two messy holes gushed blood down his back, and what was left of his head was only barely held together by the extravagant wraps of strapping tape I'd wound around it.

Finke was alive and kicking, screaming behind his gag and flailing like a man strapped to Old Sparky instead of a ninety-nine dollar Walmart office chair.

Honey remained crouched behind them with her gun raised beside her cheek, a cold and determined cast in her eyes, effectively using Finke as a human shield while she picked off his ambushing dickheads one at a time.

She was an amazing figure crouching there, cold-blooded, deadly, wickedly sexy.

I felt a warm gush of lust run through me and marveled that I should have enough blood left in my body to supply the amazing hard-on I was suddenly sporting.

Honey lowered her gun and leaned from her cover to take another shot, then flinched back behind Finke as the man in the doorway threw a shot her way.

I tore my gaze from her then, remembering the business at hand.

Out of nowhere the bird came, Mr. Blue bravely defending his mistress. He swooped down at the man in the doorway and clawed at the ugly face, ripping long divots across his cheek before taking wing to the far corner of the room.

The man sneered at Mr. Blue, finally seeing a living target that wasn't hiding behind the bound body of his boss, and took aim.

I blew the man's brains out before he got his shot.

I think that was the first clue the rest of the party had that I was still with the program.

Another of the guys Honey had taken down during those confusing first seconds had stilled. The other two dragged themselves over the threshold in a slow-motion retreat, tripping up the next wave that tried to crowd through the door. Most of the newcomers fell back to let their wounded out, and one tripped over a questing arm, falling forward, dropping his piece in an attempt to catch himself.

I heard the brittle snap as one of his arms broke, then the lusty scream of pain as he collapsed sideways onto it. His other hand scrambled for the dropped gun.

If I'd been in a more sporting mood I might have waited until he at least had the gun in hand before throwing lead into him. I was not in such a mood that night, and neither, apparently, was Honey. Our slugs hit him nearly simultaneously, mine entering his chest just below the throat, maybe exiting somewhere near his ass hole, Honey's blowing most of the top of his head all the way down into his lap.

The growing mess was considerable, the stink worse.

The newly deceased man's body lay in a loose sprawl over the legs of the retreating men, slowing them down, and for a few seconds the door was too bottlenecked to allow entry. Honey took that opportunity to stand and begin horsing the dolly/chair contraption toward my side of the room, unmindful of the grisly gruel that dribbled from Sleeping Ugly's popped top.

"*You're fucking it up,*" Miss Lizzie screamed from somewhere beyond the door. No sign of Miss Congeniality now, she was fucking furious. "*Dolts! Idiots!*"

I discovered I was not too badly hurt to stand, and joined Honey.

"Never find us," she mimicked, then began to laugh.

Woman's just as nutty as I am, I thought with some amazement. *Maybe nuttier.*

Somehow it was a comforting thought.

"Mea culpa," I said, feeling a smile creep onto my face despite the night's further complications, and as we wheeled our prisoner, the asshole who'd started the whole goddamn mess away, Mr. Blue reappeared from the rafters above my car and perched on the furniture dolly's rubberized handgrip.

"*Peek-a-boo, I see you,*" he informed us, then dropped a runny white splat in Finke's hair.

That bird was really beginning to grow on me.

My next plan was simple enough, but relied on speedy execution and my ability to find rope. It also depended on Finke being unconscious, so I punched him out again—that part was more than easy, it was fun—before tearing tape from around his torso in long and messy strips.

Of course the whole thing was probably going to be for nothing. If they stormed us again now we would be hard pressed to defend ourselves and work my goofy plan at the same time, and the human shield defense had failed me miserably already that night. I had a feeling that eventually Auntie Lizzie would just say *fuck it* and let them bang away at us. I don't think she liked her nephew very much either.

The silence outside my office was not perfect, the sound of shuffling footsteps and the murmur of angry conversation filtered in through the open door. The subtle noise kept us on guard, but also reminded us that they were busy making plans of their own. We had some time, but no idea how much.

And how many gunnies were still standing outside my office? No way to know for sure, but I thought we, mostly Honey, had cut their numbers down by half. Enough for them to abandon the original plan to overwhelm us by numbers. We'd stopped the initial banzai charge and turned them back out. Their next move wouldn't be so straightforward.

I pointed to Honey, then to the door.

"Cover me," I whispered, and she nodded, dropping into a crouch by the Ventura's open trunk, her sharp eyes and deadeye aim trained on the open door. A sporadic night breeze moved it, partially closing it.

I dragged Finke around the front of the Ventura, then slung him over my shoulder and laid him out carefully over the hood. It was impossible to be completely silent, but I made as little noise as possible. I didn't want to give my position away, didn't want to give them a reason to turn the garage door, or me, into Swiss cheese.

So far so good, now if I could find the rope I was pretty sure was somewhere in the *Random Shit* cupboard over my workbench.

"Psst!" Honey hissed, waved her free hand in my direction. "What are you doing?"

"Making a hood ornament," I said as I passed her by on the way to my workbench. I glanced back once, quickly, as I rounded the car's trunk, saw understanding and approval in her eyes and the impish set of her smile.

The idea was simple. My good ideas usually are. Tie shithead to the front of the Ventura, open the garage door, and drive like hell.

I still think it was a pretty good plan. If the need ever comes up again I plan to use it. I didn't get the chance that night. Before I reached the *Random Shit* drawer that night's final turd hit the fan.

There was a metallic wrenching sound, then the squeal of the bay door sliding upward.

I stopped, rounded on Honey, but she was just as surprised as I was. She couldn't have opened it anyway, the only remote was clipped to the Ventura's sun visor.

Nevertheless, the door rattled and shook its way upward along the loose track, and the first of Finke's remaining footmen became visible underneath it, lying on their bellies with their guns pointed toward us.

"Fuck!" I shouted and dove back behind the Ventura before they could shoot me again.

"Damnit!" Honey shouted and joined me in my hiding spot.

Predictable enough, bullets whined through the air past us, careened off the concrete floor, punched through the wall behind us. The door of my *Random Shit* cupboard exploded off its hinges. An avalanche of random junk spilled out onto the floor, a long coil of rope fell like a dead bird beside me.

"There he is," Miss Lizzie shouted. "Grab him!"

I ventured a glance around the Ventura's rear bumper and saw one of the shooters rise, advancing toward the splayed figure of Finke. I sent three quick shots at him, one catching him in the knee. He hit the ground screaming.

Honey threw shots around the other side of the Ventura, then ducked back behind the car as someone returned them.

I rose up behind the trunk in time to see Finke slide from the hood and stumble off under his own power.

I'll hit him twice next time, I thought, knowing damn well there would be no *next time*.

The thugs and morons had ferreted out my adequate, if seedy, crash pad and taken away our only leverage. We were fucked, and I knew it.

I ducked back down, looked at Honey, found her looking back at me. There was no fear in her face, only resignation.

"You are an exciting date," she paused, winked, "Rondo Hackman. A shame it has to end so soon."

"Honey." It was Finke, leader of the pack again and full of his old cockiness. "Why don't you and your new friend come out with your hands up and have a chat with us. Maybe we can work our differences out."

Low, scattered laughter from Finke's remaining men met this.

"You can go fuck yourself," Honey replied in her hateful Natasha Fatale accent.

"Mr. Hackman? Rondo?" Miss Lizzie this time. Not a hint of Finke's arrogance. She used her drawing room voice, her teatime voice. "Out of the way as we are, someone is bound to show up after all that noisome shooting. If you agree to come with us now before unwanted company arrives I'm sure we could work something out."

"Otherwise," she sighed extravagantly, "we're going to have to shoot you."

Honey rolled her eyes, remained crouched, ready for action.

How many shots did we have left between the two of us?

Not many.

"Ma'am?"

"Yes?" Miss Lizzie's voice betrayed nothing but lively interest.

I called on a collection of obnoxious and juvenile insults, selected one that had been a favorite back in my middle school days, dusted it off. "Lick me where I shit."

A sharp intake of breath from beyond the open bay door, followed by a long silence, pregnant with violence.

I had actually offended the murderous bitch.

Then the sound of an approaching car, something big and gas-guzzlingly powerful, a squeal of tires as it rounded a sharp corner, and light washed over the darkness beyond the open bay door.

A chorus of shocked expletives.

"What . . . ?" Miss Lizzie's voice was high and reedy in her shock, something more fitting of the thin humorless face on Sleeping Ugly's caller ID. She sounded a little like Mr. Blue, the crazy macaw.

I rose up and dared a peek through the Ventura's rear window. All eyes were facing the approaching light, hands shielding faces, guns pointed blindly at the approaching car. Finke staggered a little, his face pummeled and bruised, his hair matted with a weird pink icing, half blood, half guano.

"*Stop it,*" Miss Lizzie shrieked, stomping up and down like a kid having a tantrum. "*Shoot you lead-brained cock-suckers!*"

"*Shoot,*" Finke echoed.

Finke's remaining scumbags, no more than a half-dozen not including Miss Lizzie, actually got a few shots off before the car, an exquisite '53 Cadillac Eldorado convertible, plowed into them.

Scumbags flew through the air like tiddlywinks, bounced off the hood of the flamingo pink Cadi like bouncy balls. One landed in the Cadi's rear seat, all unhinged limbs and a terminally shocked face screaming blood. Miss Lizzie did a spread eagle summersault over the hood and landed, shrieking, in front of the open bay door.

Finke had dashed to the left almost in time to avoid the Cadi's front bumper altogether, instead of splatting him like a bug it clipped his leg, spinning him past his prone aunt. He glanced off the Ventura's bumper, almost fell, then caught himself on the thin tin wall, banging against it like a hammer against a gong.

The Cadillac screeched to a halt outside, the oddly sprawled figure of a man with a Sniveling Shits tank top sliding down the hood, his exposed gut squeaking against the garish pink paint like a squeegee over a dry windshield.

Somewhere over the cacophony of squealing rubber, belated gunshots, screams and groans of pain, and the single shout of rage coming from Finke's demented and bruise contorted gob, Mr. Blue screeched and sang a happy song.

Another splat of bird shit landed on the concrete between Finke and I.

The gun was still in his hand, but it was pointed at the floor. His eyes had settled on me, but were glazed, stunned.

I wasn't giving the dickhead a chance to get his marbles rolling in the right direction. I leveled my gun on him, aiming for his chest, and pulled the trigger.

There was, of course, nothing but an unsatisfying dry click. I'd fired it empty.

Finke's eyes found mine, cleared, and he smiled.

His 9mm twitched and waggled its way into the air between us until it blocked the swollen right side of his face.

He pulled the trigger.

This time there was no dry click.

The bang was large. Too large.

And for some reason, I failed to die.

A second later, I realized why.

Finke's cheap-shit 9mm with its clip of hot-loaded and lacquer-sealed bullets exploded in his hand, blowing off four of the five digits, reducing the rest of his flailing paw into hamburger.

Posey, my weapon guru, would have laughed. Hell, he might even have predicted it.

Mr. Blue landed on Finke's wrist, his beak diving into the irreparable mess.

Finke forgot about me, forgot about Honey, forgot everything but the bloody ball of white agony spouting blood from the end of a ruined arm.

He waved it, screaming, dancing in place.

"*Dickweed*," Mr. Blue screeched, and took flight again.

Finke's eyes found mine one last time, void of rage, void of recognition, void of understanding. There was only pain.

He opened his mouth to say something . . .

Bang!

. . . and fell over on his face.

John Reynolds, esquire, District Attorney of Paradise Valley, stood next to his pink Cadillac. His gun, a .357 with a short, fat barrel, was still pointed at the spot where Finke had stood. He stared down at the body for a moment, then up at me.

"Was that him? Was that . . ."

"Cameron Finke," I confirmed.

I heard sirens in the distance. The cavalry was finally on its way.

John Reynolds, local political big-bug and father of a hooker named Candy Roche, Rock Candy, stepped forward. The vapid, somehow loose set of his face contracted and tightened. Cheeks that were well on the way to jowlhood colored a blotchy red and firmed. He pointed his big gun at Cameron Finke's back and fired. He fired it empty, then dry fired another half-dozen times.

A hand slipped around my arm, gripped it tightly and pulled me back.

"I think you should leave him alone a while," Honey said in her sexy Natasha Fatale accent.

I thought that was a pretty good idea. An excellent one, in fact. I thought Mr. DA's mind had stepped out for a bit, driven into some dark cave of his psyche by shock and sadness. The fat and psychotic hate machine that stood over what was left of Cameron Finke would just as soon turn on me. His big .357 was empty, but there were other guns scattered among the dead and dying outside.

The sirens were close now.

Mr. DA stopped dry firing his gun, looked at it with some weak species of shocked recognition, then dropped it on Finke's blood-soaked back. He spat on Finke, then walked back to his car, opened the passenger door, and sat down inside.

The police were inside the gates now, the sound of screeching tires joined the warbling sirens. Red and blue washed over the carnage in stuttering flashes.

Mr. DA began to wail.

"Ah shit," I said, and allowed Honey to pull me further back into the garage portion of my office.

"They're almost here," Honey said. "Butch, come closer."

She pulled me close, very close, drew me down behind the Ventura, then pressed her lips to my ear. "You're a very interesting fellow, Butch Quick."

She kissed the lobe of my ear.

I started to melt.

"I wish we could have met under more . . . casual circumstances." Then she drew away slightly.

I could see something in her eyes that might have been half sorrow, half amusement. Frantic stomping footfalls outside. Shouting.

"I have to go now," she said.

I didn't see her raise the gun in her hand, but I saw it come down.

There was pain, the final indignity of that long, luckless night, exploding light behind my eyes, then darkness.

"Goodbye, Butch Quick."

CHAPTER 30

I didn't get much privacy over the next few days, or much sleep. By the time it was all over I looked back on that hour long stretch of unconsciousness Honey had left me as a parting gift with something like nostalgia. They didn't arrest me, but they did hold me for questioning for a couple of days until they could assemble my story, and the stories of Finke's surviving scumbags, into a more or less coherent whole. The tape I'd provided them from Officer Logan's cruiser probably helped some, Officer Friendly's plea bargaining certainly helped thin the ranks of the local PD.

Gina White's unexpected involvement helped too.

She went to bat for me, maybe out of lingering affection. We had our time together, which she ended because I couldn't put the Redwolf business behind me. To me it had never been anything more than a desperate kind of comfort. I don't know what it was for her. She'd been a victim and had learned to cope, but I never could.

I spent those restless days in Paradise Valley PD's interrogation room or sequestered in a nearby safe house. The safe house was the Hillary Hotel, the kind of tumbledown shithole where the maids cuss you out in rapid-fire Spanglish, the guy in the next room spends most of the night in violent disagreement with his television, and the cockroaches scamper right over the top of your bare feet if you're foolish enough to walk to the toilet without putting your shoes on. I can't complain too much. The room was free and my armed babysitter mostly stayed out of my hair. If not for the good opinions of John Reynolds and Gina my unpaid vacation would have been much longer and the safe house would have had lots of steel bars.

What saved me from prosecution in the end, I'm almost sure of it, wasn't that search and rescue divers found the bodies of Mr. Tattoo, the bad cop, and Candice Reynolds, plus a few bonus corpses I didn't know about, exactly where I said they would, or that I'd helped bring down a drug ring that the local law had never been quite able to get a firm grip on and highlight a wider ring of bad guys and girls that spanned the globe, but Sleeping Ugly's confession. There had been a lot of good stuff in it, and they'd been able to use a lot of it to their advantage in the following days.

There were also a lot of records, PDF documents, audio from recorded phone calls, and an extensive list of contacts on the Droid phone one of Miss Lizzie's guys had used to open my garage door.

Those Droids have an application for everything. I need to get me one of those.

My name was not on the Droid's contact list.

Neither did my name make it into the local paper, or

my face on the local television news. The can of worms I'd opened that night was still spilling over, would likely continue to do so for a long time, but all of the Paradise Valley worms were either squashed or bottled up, and none of the bottled worms knew my name. There was likely a large price on the head of the fictional Rondo Hackman, my favorite alias up in smoke, but Butch Quick would be safe enough, or as safe as he ever was.

As for Honey . . .

The fine men and women of the Paradise Valley PD did not see her leaving the scene that night, did not catch her sneaking back into her flat to pack the bare essentials before vanishing into the night like a shadow, never laid so much as a finger on her.

After bonking me on the head, Honey simply evaporated.

I haven't seen her since.

There is the postcard though.

Laughlin, Nevada at night, a dark river highlighted in the rainbow colors of casinos, a huge neon-lit riverboat called Colorado Belle—hotel and casino in one—captured in a moment of stark and decadent beauty.

The message was short and sweet.

> *Look me up some time, hero. You're an interesting date. Give*
> *Mr. Blue a kiss for me. I miss the little fellow.*
>
> *H*

I paid Mr. Blue a visit the afternoon I received that postcard. Not at Mr. DA's house, the bird had lasted less than a week in that home before his colorful vocabulary had offended one of Reynolds's important friends. His new home was at the office of Higheagle Classics.

The bird seemed happy to see me, hopped in his cage and greeted me with a cheery "*Here comes trouble!*"

"Damn straight," my uncle enthused, then laughed heartily as he thumped me on the back. "I love that bird."

"I can tell," I said.

So did I, tell the truth, but I never was very good with roommates. No reason to sour a good relationship.

"Got some work for you big boy. Bail jumper, peeping tom with an eye for the young'uns." He scooped a file folder from his cluttered desk and pressed it into my hands. "Scrawny little fellow called Leon Mears."

I tucked the folder under my arm without opening it.

"Why the hell not. Got nothing else to do"

"It's a cakewalk," my uncle assured me. "Got a good lead on his location. You'll probably be back by dark."

He patted me on the back again, surreptitiously guiding me toward his open office door. "My promise to you, big guy, nothing to worry about."

Yeah, right.

From the Misadventures of Butch Quick

I've believed a lot of dumb shit in my life, people just love to fool themselves, but some shit is too dumb even for me to swallow. Vampires, werewolves, Santa Claus, and honest politicians. Topping the list of things too outrageous for even me to buy ... zombies.

I do *not* believe in zombies.

The western sky was red fading to black, the Paradise Valley light pollution just a distant lighter haze to the north, and below me, in The Pit, the party was still pretty much under control. As under control as X raves ever were anyway. There was a lot of heavy petting and ass-grabbing masquerading as dancing, but that's X for you. At least it doesn't make you eat people's faces, like some of the new shit out there on the streets.

The Pit is one of those out of the way places that attracts partiers from time to time, an abandoned rock quarry in the hills south of the city. A stone dimple at the ass-crack end of a shit gravel road. The Pit was half a city block around and thirty feet deep, accessible by a single steep and rusting iron staircase. A few old sheds and ancient rock crushers loomed nearby to lend atmosphere, and did a nice job I thought. Part of an old conveyer gantry still jutted out over the edge of The Pit. The rest lay dismantled and scattered at the bottom.

It's not used as often these days. There's no cell reception at The Pit, and the current generation of creampuffs go to pieces without their cell phones.

I'd considered trying to keep a lookout from one of the old catwalks that seemed to hold the decaying mess together but decided against it. Just because everyone down there was stoned didn't make them blind. The guy standing at the top of the steps handing out goodie bags to the new arrivals would see me for sure, and I didn't want anyone to see me until I was ready to act. I didn't want *her* to spot me until it was too late to run away.

I'm Butch Quick, or as I'm sometimes known on the streets of Paradise Valley, that big, fuck-ugly, sasquatch-looking guy. It's an unfair comparison, since Native American's don't have that much body hair. If you're looking for the missing link, there are plenty of rednecks in Eastern Washington who fit that bill better than I do.

I don't spend all of my time sneaking around abandoned quarries to spy on ravers. I don't think I could handle it, that techno crap they play makes me want to hurt people. Mostly I repo cars and collect bail jumpers for my Uncle Higheagle, owner of Higheagle Classic Cars and Eagle Eye Bailbonds. This wasn't a normal night though. It wasn't even a normal rave.

There were lights set up around the perimeter of The Pit, one pointing down from the catwalk above the rock crushers, another pointed down from a crumbling outcrop on the far side, probably a few more I couldn't see from where I sat with the binoculars. The lights were still dark, the only light came from a bonfire down in The Pit.

The partiers below me, the ones who hadn't already stripped naked – that X just seems to bring out the naked in some people – were dressed up as zombies.

A zombie themed rave in an old-school horror movie setting.

I was in the right place, now it was just a matter of waiting for the right time and keeping my eyes peeled for The Director and his fresh young starlet.

Vikki Greene.

They arrived just when I was beginning to second-guess myself.

A small U-Haul rolled up and parked alongside the clusterfuck of rust bucket vans, pickups, and cars. The girl who hopped down from the passenger side was a slightly older and punkier version of the girl from my photo. She wore tight black pants and a muscle shirt. Bright red hair stuck up in sporty spikes around a pale, pixyish face. She was smiling, bouncing with each step. Excited.

The Director came around the other side and joined her a moment later.

He was an older guy, stocky, blocky, his gray hair buzz-cut and his face clean-shaven. Dressed in a crisp black suit. Not exactly what I'd expected, more than a bit out of place. He looked like a banker or lawyer, except for the cane he carried, black with a skull for a handle. It looked ornamental rather than functional. He rolled the U-Haul's back door up and motioned toward the leaning shacks at the pit's edge.

Three guys rushed from the darkness inside the nearest shack, next to the edge of The Pit, and scrambled inside. They came out a minute later packing a camera, a big one on a tall tripod, and what looked like a lot of antique studio recording equipment.

They carried their load of shit back into the shed, and a few minutes later I heard the distant rumble of a generator. The spotlights joined the bonfire at the center of the pit, stuttering and flashing like strobes, and the ravers cheered when the lights fell on them. It gave the whole event the texture of an LSD nightmare, techno music and raving zombies in a Stone Age discotheque.

The men collected short stacks of bills from The Director and bags of party supplies from Mr. Goodie Bags, high-fived each other and joined the fun below.

Vikki waited by the U-Haul, bouncing with anticipation. Ready to get the show started. The Director took her by the arm and she settled to listen to him. He pointed down into The Pit with the point of his cane and made lots of very cirectorial hand gestures.

Maybe they were discussing motivation and subtext.

She was on her way, Mr. Goodie Bags didn't offer her any of his chemical music enjoyment enhancers as she passed him by, and a minute later she was lost in the crowd.

The Director disappeared around the far side of the old shacks and appeared again a few seconds later climbing a dangerous looking spiral staircase that led up the catwalks.

There was no call of *Action*, but I thought the show had started. Maybe not a porn movie after all, which would be a relief to Vikki's old man. Still, she was sixteen, and The Director had encouraged her to run away from home to star in this cheap-ass movie of his.

He was damn lucky Vikki's old man hadn't wanted to get the law involved.

Which was why I was there.

I decided to sit back and wait it out, give The Director a chance to shoot his zombie flick, then follow them after the party broke up. Grab the girl when there weren't fifty or so ravers standing between us.

A few minutes later the screaming started down in The Pit, and my plan was shot to hell.

Thad Greene was an old acquaintance, not quite a friend, whose company I was too often forced to endure out of obligation to my then girlfriend and future wife, Beth Trout. Thad's younger sister was one of Beth's best friends, and Thad was an unrepentant tag along. I never cared for the guy much, but I don't care for most people.

Thad Greene was a pompous and upwardly mobile kiss-ass who majored in business management and had a five-year plan to marry rich so he'd never have to apply his education in the real world. Like him or not, you have to give him some credit. His five-year plan had worked, and he'd managed it in only three years. By graduation he was engaged to a cute little-miss-money-bags who smoked a lot of dope, dressed like a '60s hippy, and drove her daddy's hand-me-down Beamer. She was the youngest sister of Paradise Valley's currently reigning District Attorney, the spoiled baby-girl of the well monied Reynold's family.

I didn't see him much after college until Paradise Valley's very own serial killer, Redwolf, killed my wife and daughter. Thad's brother-in-law tried his hardest to hang the crime on me, and Thad got his own fifteen minutes of fame when he appeared on the news. He screamed for my blood and pumped out the tears in an academy award-worthy performance that the local press ate up. They still play those clips from time to time, whenever Redwolf makes the news again.

So, when he called me at just after nine that Saturday morning I quite naturally suggested he fuck off and die. I may have even offered to help him before I hung up. He called back, and I hung up again. On his third callback I realized it would be easier to just let him talk, and that was when he laid his sob story on me.

Sucker that I am, I swallowed it.

We met face to face for the first time in years an hour later, and you should be proud of me, I didn't even *try* to hit him.

I was between cars at the time and using my Uncle Higheagle's favorite showroom eye candy, a restored 1927 Indian Ace, to get around. It was a beautiful machine, scarlet red with gold striping. A bit on the small side for a large guy like me, the poor machine seemed almost to cringe away every time I hoisted my seven foot, three hundred pound frame onto it, but it was damn fun to drive.

Uncle Higheagle had reluctantly allowed me to borrow it, and his threat of a slow and painful death if I did anything bad to it sounded only half serious.

I had most of Main Street to myself, a slow Saturday morning downtown, and saw Thad before he saw me. I found a handy spot a few feet from where he sat and parked.

"Butch," he said. He put out his hand, then seemed to think better of it and dropped it to his side. "You're looking … uh, good."

He took in my face, the new scars and marks on it since the last time he'd seen it up close, and cringed back a step.

I indicated my disinterest in continued small talk.

"Cut the shit, Greene. What have you got for me?"

He blushed and took his seat.

We'd decided to meet on neutral ground. He suggested Starbucks. I vetoed it and told him to meet me at Greasy's Grill, a little place on Main Street in the east valley. Good food but a cramped dining room. I preferred to sit at the table outside on the sidewalk, which was where Thad was waiting.

It was a favorite of Beth's.

Not sure why I picked the place, I'm not normally given to nostalgia.

I took the seat across from him at the outside table and eyed his cup of coffee with a pang of jealousy.

He wasted no more time on small talk, slapped a sheath of folded pages down on the table between us.

"Butch, please help me. I know that I've …," and there he seemed to lose his guts again.

I decided to help out.

"You said I was a monster and called for my blood on national television," I said. "I remember. The clips are on YouTube."

"Butch, please. It's my daughter."

I reached across the table and he flinched back again. I took his cup of coffee and finished it off in a gulp, then took the stack of printed pages and unfolded them. Figured if I was going to accept this ridiculous chore I might as well get started.

I ordered another coffee and read what he'd given me. Some social media chatter and private messages between Thad's daughter, sixteen-year-old wild child Vikki, and a guy who called himself The Director. Then emails.

"Have you tried having his email address traced?" Simple stuff, and not one of my skills.

"Yes," he said. "The address is rerouted through random nodes, scrambled. Completely anonymous."

Whatever the hell that means, I thought.

I went back to the emails and spent the next several minutes being a semiprofessional snoop.

In a nutshell, bored, over-privileged teenage girl meets creepy, and apparently anonymous independent film director online. Cue the slightly inappropriate relationship. Girl flirts a little and director compliments her on her obvious star quality. Things continue in that vein for a few months, then The Director tells her he's coming to Paradise Valley to shoot a new movie, a zombie flick he expects to be the next big breakaway.

Like The Blair Witch Project with raving zombies, he said, and *I'd like you to play the lead, if you're up to it.*

Her reply: *Fuck me 'till I cry … hell yeah!*

The last email from The Director the previous Wednesday: *On my way now. Will call you when I'm in town. Can't wait to meet you, Vikki. You're gonna be a star!*

I refolded the sheets and set them down.

Next he handed me a photograph, a year or so out of date, but unless she'd done something drastic to her colorful appearance it would be good enough. I'd have no trouble recognizing the real life Vikki if I spotted her.

"And what makes you think I can find her?" I already knew the answer but I wanted to hear him say it. I felt for him a little, I knew what it was like to lose a child. But he was a still an asshole.

He squirmed a little, blushed again.

"Because you know … people. You have connections." He was unexpectedly tactful. Then he said something that actually surprised me. "And you're smart about stuff like this. I've heard stories."

"From your good old brother-in-law?" The fact that DA Reynolds had once tried to have me locked up for life hadn't stopped him from getting mixed up in one of my more memorable misadventures.

Thad regarded his hands sitting on the table with apparent interest and nodded.

Having a reputation sucks. People always expect you to live up to it.

"Listen, Butch, she's only sixteen." His blush went a shade deeper, anger trumping embarrassment. "I don't know what this guy has in mind for her but it can't be good!"

I had a pretty good idea. I'm sure he did too. There may or may not be zombies involved, but creepy anonymous director plus rebellious sixteen-year-old girl says porn to me.

I pushed the folded sheets and photograph back to him.

"Call the cops. Sic your brother-in-law on him. This is their job, not mine."

"I can't." He spoke quietly and seemed to shrink a few inches on his seat. "She's been in too much trouble already, and ..."

"*And what?*" My irritation was growing. My self-improving resolution not to hit the guy was getting harder to keep.

"If this gets out to the press ... shit, I have to keep this quiet. We can't have another scandal in the family now."

I took a few moments to absorb this, to try to rationalize around the obvious subtext. I couldn't.

"You don't want to embarrass the rich relatives," I said. "You're afraid your little girl will make them look bad and they'll punish you for it. Pull you off the cash cow's tit?"

Thad said nothing.

"You're a real piece of work," I said.

"What do you want," Thad asked. "How much for you to find Vikki and bring her back to me?"

"I can't guarantee ...," I started, and Thad cut me off.

"I know, goddamnit! I know!" Heads inside Greasy's turned toward us. A professorial looking fellow, lots of tweed and gray hair, a pipe dangling from the corner of his mouth and a pair of spectacles perched on the end of his nose, gave us a very disapproving look as he passed. "Just do what you can!"

He didn't believe a word he was saying. In his mind it was a done deal. He cuts a check and I bring his girl back. A simple transaction that I was fucking up with semantics.

I named my price, a pretty outrageous one I thought.

He cut the check without a second's hesitation.

Well shit, now I was freelancing as a private investigator.

Thad Greene was right about one thing. I did know people.

I also knew a walking modern art exhibit named Boswell.

"Quick! The fuck you doin' Chief!" Boswell seemed happy to hear from me, which is not always the case with people. Our first encounter brought a bit of extra excitement, not to mention a pack of armed lunatics, into one of his nightly raves, and apparently he had enjoyed it quite a bit.

Boswell was a local dealer and lunatic who hosted nightly raves in an unused warehouse basement. He favored chain mail and leather clothing. Every available inch of flesh was inked or pierced, and he wore his hair in foot-long spikes. Boswell sold a shitload of X to his ravers, but he kept them off the streets, and that was something.

"Still breathing." I caught myself smiling. Boswell was a scumbag dealer and a bit freaky for my taste, but he was a likable freaky scumbag dealer. "You still in business?"

"Hell yeah I'm still in business!" Talking to Boswell was an adventure. You had to brace yourself for every reply. "You gonna grace us with your presence again? I didn't think that was your scene."

"You guys are too wild for me," I said. "But you keep your ear to the ground, right? You'd know if there's another party going on?"

"Abso-fucking-lutely, Chief! "Whatchu lookin' for?"

"Zombies," I said, and managed not to laugh at myself.

Boswell did laugh. "That sounds wild, Chief! Maybe I'll do that for Halloween!"

"Nothing like that going down any time soon then?"

"News to me if there is," he said, settling back into normal conversation.

I was about to thank him and hang up when he said, "If you're not stuck on the whole zombie thing there is something big going down tonight at The Pit, and that place hasn't seen heavy action in years."

"There is?" It wasn't exactly gold, but maybe I'd struck something.

"Zero shit my man. You know The Pit, right?"

I knew The Pit.

The screaming started, a single hysterical high-pitched voice ringing out impressively over the rotten tooth throb of bad techno music. I snapped out of the semi-doze I'd been drifting into and scanned the jumble of bouncing bodies, a few more naked now and more stripping down even as I watched. A second scream sounded and I found the screamer, a bald chick in black bra, panties, and combat boots was doing a really excellent job pretending to be bitten by a naked man in zombie makeup, splattered with fake blood.

I zoomed in on them and was impressed by the man's ferocity and the spray of fake arterial blood as he ripped a chunk of flesh free from her neck. The spray fanned out and drenched the ravers closest to them. More screams, as if that had been their mark.

I'm not a big fan of the zombie genre, but I could give credit where it was due. Even with a stoned all amateur cast and the shoestring budget the setup suggested, The Director made it convincing.

Too convincing maybe, because the panic that spread out from the pair, zombie and victim in a blood drenched death struggle, was real.

When the raver in the zombie makeup went for the bald girl again and tore most of her right cheek off with his teeth, I realized that was real too.

While I was trying to work out just what the fuck was happening below, more screams sounded around The Pit. More attacks, more blood, and now there were a half-dozen zombie ravers bearing down on a half-dozen victims.

Vikki stood in the middle of it all, scared but keeping her cool, then began forcing herself through any gap she could make, fighting her way slowly back toward the steps.

I pointed my binoculars at the top of the steps, at the man with the goodie bags, saw him intercept the first panicky young man to reach the top. Mr. Goodie Bags pulled a small pistol from the waistband of his pants and poped the guy in the face.

The man flew off his feet and slammed into the people

packed in behind him. The forward surge up the steps became a domino tumble back to the bottom. One of the tumbling bodies, a pretty Latino girl dressed in the height of zombie fashion, convulsed when she hit the bottom. When one of her friends tried to help her up she raked with her fingers and snapped at the helping hand with bared teeth.

More wildly dancing figures tumbled to the dirt. Eyes rolled, foam frothed from grinning lips.

Down in The Pit, shit was getting real.

More gunfire.

From high above on the old catwalks, The Director watched, hands on hips.

Behind me, hidden off-road, was the old Indian Ace and the glow of Paradise Valley. Ahead was The Pit, a whole lot of crazy, and one gullible sixteen-year-old girl I'd agreed to return to her family.

I had to pick a direction, and damn quick.

I do not believe in zombies.

What I did believe in was good old fashioned human fuckery. *That* I'd seen proven time and again.

I picked a direction and ran.

Guess which direction I picked.

As I've said, the old Indian was a favorite of My Uncle's, another old Indian, and the young Indian riding it was going to get his ass kicked if he cracked it up. I tried to put that out of my mind as I rode full throttle toward the sound of techno and screaming.

This is usually the point at which I'll cobble together

some god-awful Rube Goldberg style exit strategy. This time I gave it a pass and decided to play it by ear.

I do not believe in zombies.

Mr. Goodie Bags was my immediate problem. He was the one with the gun.

The old rock crushers loomed into view, backlit by the glow of the flashing lights and the bonfire blazing in The Pit. I could see a speck up in the catwalks, The Director overseeing his current masterpiece no doubt, and then I was weaving through the jumble of cars and trucks. A second later Mr. Goodie Bags turned my way, the grin on his face withering when he registered the giant Indian zooming toward him.

He raised his gun and fired. The wind from his first slug tugged at my shirtsleeve, the second pinged off the front wheel guard. My uncle was going to skin me for that. The third didn't even come close.

He screamed as I plowed into him and sent him flying up and over the jumble of bodies on the steps. He hit the chaos below and disappeared in a mass of bodies, some still dancing, oblivious to the deadly dance going on around them, some attempting to climb over the bodies piled in front of them.

The flashing lights and screaming made the scene feel even more like a bad acid trip than ever, unreal but still dangerous.

Was I really about to throw myself down into that mess?

I spotted Vikki again, near the center and working her way toward the steps.

A few more zombies, or whatever the hell they were, pounced and tore at wide-eyed, Xed out ravers. More bodies hit the ground convulsing, either from the strobe lights or the shit Mr. Goodie Bags gave them.

One of the chompers, a big gruesome fucker in threadbare cutoffs and metal mixing bowl helmet was bearing down on Vicki. He looked like an undead Viking, a lot of long, dirty blonde hair, a long, braided beard that wagged energetically with each stride he took, thick mustache and face dripping with blood.

A red-faced fat guy dripped with sweat and tore at his T-shirt. His scream was silent in the overall racket. When the shirt was gone he tore at the skin of his bulging belly.

Young people these days, with their raves and techno music and drug-induced zombie rampages ... they make my generation look almost sane and respectable.

I twisted the old Indian's throttle and went over the edge with a slight whimper of anticipation. The ride down those rusted metal steps was quick and bumpy, like a jackhammer to the nuts. I consoled myself by causing even more havoc as I rode down toward the bottleneck at the bottom.

Most scattered. A few who'd made it through the bottleneck bailed over the handrails. The ones still in my path were either bleeding out or foaming. One ran up to meet me with a gurgle of rage, and I amused myself further by running him down. There was a moment when I thought I was going to end up on my head, this was not an off-road bike and I was about as off-road as I could get, but I kept it upright and hit the bottom of The Pit with great relief and a burst of speed.

So far so good, and no one else was trying to shoot me yet.

The path ahead of me emptied rapidly, those still

mostly in their right minds giving me plenty of room. Those who didn't ... well, I was here to rescue one girl, not save every brain-blasted fuck-wit who'd turned up as an extra in The Director's movie, a zombie themed snuff film made on a shoestring budget and some really mean street pharmaceuticals.

Most were getting away now, leaving the foamers and chompers behind to focus their attention on the biggest and noisiest distraction in The Pit.

Me.

I spotted Vikki in the thinning crowd. She was on the ground, pushing herself away from the Viking.

He loomed over her, shaking and shambling, his face splitting in a bloody grin.

I do not believe in zombies.

And to prove it to myself, I aimed the Indian at him and twisted the throttle.

We hit with a crunch and he flew backward and landed in a sprawl.

The Indian reared up and threw me in a sprawl next to him.

Before I could shake off the tumble and rise, the chompers were surrounding me.

I do not believe in zombies, but these guys were going to have a try at changing my mind. The first one bent, lunged, and I kicked his feet out from under him. The second and third went for me, a stubby little guy in skid-marked briefs and a pretty little thing with a blue mohawk and a nose ring the size of a door knocker. I knocked most of the guy's teeth out, but hesitated when the girl came at me. My uncle had raised me not to hit girls. No exceptions.

This one bit though, and really fucking hard.

I shook her off as the next one went for me, a scrawny guy in baggy black pants, a torn net shirt, and a lot of bad jailhouse ink.

He grinned and leaned down toward me as two others grabbed hold of my arms and bit. I brought their heads together with a satisfying smack and they hit the dirt twitching.

Almost on my feet, The Pit nearly empty now, the ravers split and the chompers scattering in search of easier pickings, when the dickweed in the net shirt grabbed me by the throat and went for my face with his broken and bloodied teeth.

There was a clang, blood trickled from his greasy mop of hair, and he tipped over sideways.

Vikki stood there, holding the long handle of a flat edged shovel in her hands like a baseball bat. She looked pleased with herself.

"An Indian riding an Indian," she said. "Gotta love the irony."

I did a quick dust off while she crouched in a menacing manner with her shovel. Another chomper charged us and she whacked him in the face with the flat of the shovel's head.

A hurried moment later I mounted Uncle Higheagle's old Indian and Vikki jumped onto the seat behind me. I spun a quick circle, almost mandatory when making a desperate escape on a cool motorbike, and threw a rooster tail of gravel at a fat, lurching chomper. He cried out, threw his hands over his face, stumbled off in another direction.

Vikki whooped, clearly enjoying herself.

I found the steep steps to the slightly saner world outside The Pit and went for it.

Vikki shouted something unintelligible at me. Between the echoing roar of the Indian and the warbling syntho-screeching of the music, normal communication was out, but when I turned my head to her I found a finger pointing at two o'clock near The Pit's far wall. Two lady chompers advanced on a skinny little guy who looked like Justin Beiber in cargo pants, suspenders, and not much else. His back was to the granite and he raised his arms over his face to block the approaching menace.

I got the idea and turned toward them. It was against my deeply ingrained personal code to hit women, even the ones who bit from time to time, but Vikki was free to wallop whoever the hell she wanted. She did so with obvious relish, hanging onto the back of my shirt with one hand, gripping the shovel's handle high up with the other.

Her swing was short, but momentum was on her side. She knocked the closest lady chomper off her feet, and when the other turned our way with a snarl, the Justin Beiber look-alike made a run for it.

"*More!*" Vikki screamed, and I obliged. I drove twice around The Pit, veering close enough to the menacing chompers to give Vikki a swing, and she swatted them like flies. One fell backward against a rusted oil drum where a battery powered boom-box blasted that shitty techno. It fell to the dirt, ejected the CD and switched to a local FM station. The Ramones belted out *I Wanna Be*

Sedated and improved my mood considerably. She knocked another into the bonfire, where he flailed and screamed and sent sparks up in a cyclone.

I decided to get the fuck out while we were still capable of getting and turned the Indian back toward the steps.

I wasn't exactly happy with the night's work, there were too many bodies in the dirt to call my intervention a success, too many crazed chompers still nibbling on them, but I'd earned my paycheck. Vikki was safe and apparently enjoying herself, and most of the hapless fuck-nuts who'd shown up for this fun little get-together were running or driving away.

I saw Goodie Bags crouched under the steps.

Goodie Bags saw us coming, and stepped out to greet us. He'd found his gun and pointed it at us.

I jigged left and avoided his first shot, right and avoided the second. I was close enough when he aimed again that he couldn't have missed, but he'd fired his big revolver dry. I buzzed by close on his left and Vikki swung her shovel like a pro.

He went down flat on his back and a few lonely chompers jumped on the chance to get some face time with him.

"More!" Vikki screamed. "This is fucking fun!"

I'd had enough *fun* for one night though and gunned it up the steps

This second helping of the jackhammer to the nuts experience was muted slightly by the collection of bites and bruises I'd picked up, and Vikki had to drop her chomper club to hold on with both hands.

A wild half minute later we were on flat ground again,

and I was about to let myself experience a bit of relief when The Ramones ended and The Director shouted down at me from his high place in the catwalk above the old rock crushers. I wanted to get down the road, back to town and relieve myself of my teenage passenger, but I was curious to hear what he had to say. I stopped and searched the catwalks above until I found him.

He stood behind one of the flashing lights. He was too far away for me to see the smile on his face, but I could hear it in his voice.

"Holy shit! What'a show!" The Director seemed ecstatic, overjoyed at the unexpected turn of events. "Excellent improvising … and what a face! You were made to be in horror movies!"

"You're a fucking asshole!" Vikki jumped off the back of the bike and started toward the crusher. "You tried to kill me!"

"Yes," The Director said. "And I'm going to be a rich asshole! This is going to sell a million copies!"

He laughed and danced in place.

Regretting my curiosity now. "Vikki, get back here."

She ignored me and I reluctantly dismounted to follow her.

"I'm going to call it …," The Director spread his arms wide and stared up into the night sky. *"Zombie A-Go-Go: Dancing With The Dead!"*

"Fuck your movie," Vikki shouted back up at him, and ran toward the nearest shack. The makeshift studio.

"No!" The Director screamed. "Don't go in there!"

She ignored him and sprinted toward the gaping hole in the side of the shack that used to be a door.

The Director screamed and jumped up and down like

a toddler having a tantrum, then ran down the catwalk, toward the spiraling steps that led back to the ground, waving his prop cane over his head.

A quick check around showed a mostly deserted parking lot: a half-dozen rust buckets of varying make and model, The Director's U-Haul, and my Indian. The groans and screams from inside The Pit were tapering off. The Director's chompers seemed to have run out of juice. Now there was only The Director, Vikki, and me.

And whatever new surprises The Director might have up his sleeves.

I decided not to give him the chance to surprise us again.

I ran past the shack, where Vikki was energetically smashing equipment, and found the dizzying twist of steps.

I got a good look down into The Pit as I climbed, saw the dead and injured, the wound-down chompers looking almost as pathetic as their victims. A familiar slow burn started in my guts, a mostly unwelcome sensation that meant I was about to lose my temper and do something very antisocial. I usually try to squash the rage before it blooms, but this time I let it come. I welcomed it back like the old and troublesome friend it was. I decided to close down The Director's little operation for good.

I heard a final smash below followed by Vikki's laughter, The Director's hurried footfalls from above and my own heavy breathing as I stomped up the stairs. I reached the top and found The Director waiting for me in the stuttering discotheque lights.

He lurched forward, his cane raised over his head, and I dodged his first swing, almost falling over the rickety railing. He hit the handrail instead of my noggin, and I looked up in time to see him raise the cane again. The strobing lights made him look like a figure from an old film, a gaudy black and white silent movie psycho.

He scowled, screamed, swung the skull-topped cane down at me. I caught it on the downswing with one hand. It hurt, but not as much as what I did to him next.

"You big dumb oaf!" He shrieked at me. "I have to stop her! She's ruining my movie!"

I considered informing him that I didn't *have* to do shit, and decided to let my actions speak for me. Letting go of his cane, I stepped forward, reached down, grabbed a handful of his crotch with my right hand and his throat with my left. He squealed in pain as I gently heaved him up and over the catwalk's old rusty railing.

The Director's descent into The Pit was mostly silent. There was a lot of useless arm flapping and kicking, quite comical, but only a brief squawk just before he hit, as if he had only just realized it wasn't a part of his script, that it was for real. There would be no second takes.

A few of the livelier chompers scuttled over to him and began to do what they did best.

The flush of anger began to drain from my face, and I started to feel ashamed of myself. I always went too far when I lost my temper. Shit like this was the reason I had my unwanted reputation.

Screw 'im, I thought. *He had that coming.*

I took the downward steps slowly, and by the time I reached dirt I mostly felt okay about it. He wouldn't be making more of his shitty movies now.

I found Vikki standing beside the Indian Ace, The

Director's laptop closed under one arm, a satisfied grin on her face.

"That was fucking awesome," she said. "You should have told me you were doing that! I could have filmed it!"

"I can drag him back up and throw him over again," I said.

Vikki, clearly immune to my sarcasm, almost bobbed with excitement. "Would you?"

A scream broke the tense silence and Vikki spun at the sound. I turned in time to see the Viking coming at me but not quickly enough to do anything about it. He hit me like a sweaty side of beef, still screaming, and drove me into the ground. I had an easy fifty pounds on the guy, but he was insane with whatever crazy shit Goodie Bags had set them up with for the party. Sure as shit not X.

He pressed his face up against mine and for a crazy moment I thought he was trying to kiss me. That might have been preferable. He snapped at my nose and I snapped my head to the side in time to avoid losing it. We grappled for a moment. I smashed his nose and he bit my hand. I head-butted him and got another bite on the brow. He forced his face down toward my neck, teeth snapping, and I kneed him in the crotch.

A handy FYI for everyone reading this, a zombie-viking's nuts are just as vulnerable and sensitive as the next guy's. Remember that. Might come in handy someday.

The Viking groaned and seemed to lose interest in the fight, so I took the opportunity to put a few feet between us. Vikki finished it for me with a nicely placed crack to the cranium that would have caved his skull in if not for his mixing bowl helmet. He hit the ground and began to snore.

Vikki stood, regarding him with the discarded shovel back in her hands and the first hint of boredom on her face. "You know, I'm kind of bored with this shit. I don't even like zombies."

It was as good a time as any to scram, so we did.

I drove the old Indian Ace back toward town with Vikki seated behind, The Director's laptop pressed between us.

"Who are you anyway?" She yelled in my ear.

"Your father sent me looking for you." I wasn't sure how she'd greet that bit of info, but I was reasonably confident that she wasn't going to bail at 45 miles per hour however much she hated him.

There was a long moment of silence, then, *"so you're a friend of the old dickhead's?"*

"I wouldn't call the old dickhead a friend," I shouted back.

"Then why did you come for me?"

Because I'm an idiot, while factual, was too hard to admit aloud, so I lied.

"Because I'm nice!"

The Paradise Valley PD, with a few exceptions, would have been happy to toss me back into The Pit with the remaining chompers, or a cozy holding cell at the very least. It's not an attitude I like, but I'm used to it by now. They'd seen too much of me over the years, and you know what they say about familiarity. But after interviewing

Vikki and reviewing the evidence on The Director's laptop they had to let me go.

Of course a nice cozy holding cell might have been my best short term option considering the state I'd brought Uncle Higheagle's bike back in. It was still running, but I'd knocked a lot of the pretty off of it.

"I think it looks more … rugged this way," I offered as my uncle stood next to me in the Higheagle Classic Cars lot.

He didn't say anything for a long time.

I was about to start backing slowly away when he grabbed hold of my arm and examined one of the freshly bandaged bite marks. "Are you sure those weren't real zombies?"

"Uncle, there's no such thing as zombies." The zombie outbreak had been limited to a few dozen who The Director and Goodie Bags had dosed with a new street drug they called Rave. The initial effects were indistinguishable from X, the euphoria, the urge to get naked and rub up against anyone who strayed too close. Then nausea, confusion, a rapid rise in body temperature, and severe paranoia. The bloodlust that followed was a purely chemical reaction, a kind of misfiring of synapses in the prefrontal cortex. Nothing supernatural, just a bunch of drugged up degenerates dancing to bad music. A typical Saturday night in Paradise Valley in other words.

"Too bad," Uncle Higheagle said, and dropped my arm. "It would have been a good excuse to shoot you."

I don't like bringing my work home with me. I've made that mistake before with damn near fatal consequences that I wouldn't like to repeat. Which is why any job that brings me to the port district makes me nervous, and more so if that job happens to be on Port Street, the charming little slice of Paradise Valley where I lay my battered and lumpy head to rest at night.

Not that my home is anything special. For me, home is a crappy little cracker box rental cabin on a street lined with more of the same, a scuzzy urban showcase where dealers and crack whores peddle their junk and dirty kids play in yards overflowing with weeds and beer cans. But it *was* home, and if I couldn't feel safe there, then I might as well live under the piers of Redwolf Bridge with the rest of the homeless.

My target wasn't a neighbor; he lived a few blocks east of my cracker box, but he was still too close for my comfort.

I cruised around the block in my new ride, a 1970

Dodge Charger, midnight blue with black interior, marking the foot traffic around the target house. The new car was a bit bulkier than the Mustang convertible I've been coveting since boyhood, but more accommodating to my own bulky self. A seven-foot tall man must choose his transportation with care if he wants to avoid eating his own knees. I loved my old Ventura, but it was toast now, cruising that great drag strip in the sky.

A damn shame, that Ventura was one tough car, but the Charger has a certain something about it that I'm digging. The rear passenger seat is my designated bad-boy seat, fitted with restraints and covered with a tough canvas cover. Don't want some bail jumping numb-nuts crapping up my new wheels.

I parked it a few lots down and watched the house for a few minutes. No one new came, no one left. A grubby little snot rocket next door forgot the hole he was digging and watched me.

The house was larger than most in that neighborhood, which wasn't saying much. It was also a lot more squalid, which said a lot. It was old, filthy, painted an ancient and dusty pink that was peeling away from the old siding in large sheets. It was two stories renovated into a funky duplex. The bottom floor, accessible from the barren front yard, appeared empty. A hazardous looking staircase crawled up the east side of the house to a patio and upper level entrance, which was very obviously occupied. The occupants broadcasted bass-heavy rap music through their open windows to the neighborhood at large.

There were raised voices, I could hear them just below the music. They weren't happy voices. One of them could have been his voice, but it was impossible to be sure sitting below in my car.

Might as well get it over with.

I stepped out, crossed the road, stepped over half a dead cat in the gutter. Its head was cracked open and its brains were drying on the pavement. An approaching ice-cream truck rounded the corner on Port Drive and tweeted its cheerful calliope music at me.

The kid watched me with bland interest and stood when I passed his yard.

"Hey mister." He wiped a gooey wad of dust caked snot from under his nose. "Can I have a buck for ice-cream?"

"No." I was keeping an eye on the upper floor of the pink house, watching for a face in the window or the second story door to open.

"Well fuck you then," the boy said, and resumed digging his hole.

The music in the pink house continued to thump, but the voices had stopped.

The steps were sturdier than they looked, a bit of good luck I never could have predicted. I took it as a good sign and proceeded.

My name is Butch Quick, repo man, bail bond recovery agent, etc, and I have to be honest … I wasn't enjoying myself near as much as I used to when going out and about to round up potentially dangerous lowlife junkie assholes. The new crop of Paradise Valley criminals currently making their way through Eagle Eye Bail Bonds via the new and improved Paradise Valley PD were slightly less fun-loving than the previous year's models. Ever since my highly amusing misadventure with the Finkes, an organization family that controlled most of the vice, and more than a few of the cops in Paradise Valley until a few months ago, the local fuzz-nuts were bringing in some very nasty characters.

District Attorney Reynolds, who seemed to have dropped fifty pounds and put on about fifteen years since I'd last seen him, was appearing on the local news with some frequency now. He had the edifying job of explaining to a highly pissed off public that the rise in violent crime was due to a vacuum created when local and federal law enforcement effectively shut down organized crime in The Valley. In a quote that was still getting lots of play Reynolds had said *Disorganized crime has stepped in to fill the void*, and that they were working double-time to round the new bad guys up.

He had very thoughtfully left my name out of it. The Feds had put what was left of the Finke family in a pretty serious time out, but that didn't mean there wasn't a big juicy hit out on me. I'm sure they still had friends on the streets. I'd shown a bit of rare good sense and used my favorite alias with them, so good old fictional Rondo Hackman was a hunted man, but I was probably safe enough.

Well, as safe as I ever was.

If you have no idea what I'm talking about then you've clearly come late to the game.

A few months back a routine repo job went sideways and got me into a seriously fucked up game of Drugstore Cowboys and Indians. To summarize, I found the dead body of DA Reynolds's wayward daughter in the trunk of a sweet old Mustang I repossessed from local lowlife and deadbeat customer, Cameron Finke. I spent the rest of that night dodging bullets from Cameron and his boys, and insults from the second on Cameron Finke's most wanted list, the lovely and dangerous Honey Beloi.

We survived. Cameron Finke and most of his friends didn't, and what was left of them would probably like nothing more than to stick my head on a pool cue. My friend on the inside, FBI Special Agent Gina White, was making sure they never got a chance, and thank God for that. Life sucked enough when people *weren't* trying to kill me.

With the Finke's organization shut down the common Paradise Valley street scum had a bit more room to stretch their legs, and were making life a little less pleasant for the rest of us. The newly cleaned out Paradise Valley PD was doing an excellent job bringing the ambitious new crop of criminals in, and were running out of room for the lesser lowlifes.

Eagle Eye Bail Bonds was doing a booming business, and I was much busier reeling in my Uncle Higheagle's bail jumpers than usual.

The thing that made me most uncomfortable is that I *seemed* to be getting better at my job. I haven't been beaten up or shot at for quite a while. I didn't trust it. I figured I was due for a serious ass kicking any day now.

I mounted the steps as quietly as I could, abandoning my usual straightforward approach. Maybe I caught a bad vibe from inside, maybe I was just feeling extra paranoid.

Probably it was because the guy I was after was bug-fuck crazy.

Also, the shouting had stopped. Whatever was going on in there had ended abruptly.

I stepped onto the landing, put my fist out to knock, then stopped. Whatever alarm bell was going off in my head was dinging a bit harder now. There was a single window on the east side of the upper apartment, covered with aluminum foil to keep out the sun and too curious eyes. I waited for a moment, watched the door, then saw the knob begin to turn.

I reached for the little Ruger LC9 in my right pocket, my constant companion for these troublesome head-hunting jobs, changed my mind and grabbed the item in my left, one of my favorite new toys, one I prefer in a close-up confrontation.

The door opened and a scrawny man in tattered boxer shorts flew out at me, raising a cracked and splintered baseball bat over his head. His hair was crew cut, his pale skin covered with tattoos, one eye mostly swollen shut and fresh bruises covering most of his face. He screamed as his bare feet carried him over the threshold and out into the sunlight.

I don't know how he expected me to react, probably thought I'd show him my backside and zip down the steps as fast as my big feet would carry me. He wasn't quick enough with his swing though, and I take my breaks where I can get them. I'm not a proud man. I stepped forward and jabbed him between his hairy nipples with the prongs of the handy little Wasp I kept ready for just such occasions. I'd picked up this little beauty after someone else had used it on me to good effect, and it's come in handy, I can tell you. Several thousand volts of *Fuckin' Owch* in a handsome, yellow handheld wand.

I love the crackling sound it makes almost as much as the thud of an electrified body hitting then floor. I usually have to wait a bit for all the theatric twitching and flopping around to settle, but even they have to admit it's better than a slug in the gut.

I still wasn't enjoying the job as much as I should. The jack-o-lantern faced junkie flopping like a fish in the open door wasn't the man I'd come to see, and the only other person I could see was the strawberry lounging naked on a seam-split beanbag. If my target had been in the apartment, he would not have been hiding.

I didn't like dead ends, they felt like a giant waste of time, and this was starting to look an awful lot like a dead end.

But there I was, and I definitely had their attention now. Didn't hurt to ask.

"Butch Quick, Eagle Eye Bail Bonds," I flashed the badge hidden behind the hem of my shirt. "I'm looking for Laurence Gerbert."

The strawberry lost interest and decided to nod off for a while. From the color of her skin and the purple around her eyes I guessed she was on the ass end of long dopamine ride, and crashing hard.

Her supplier was coming around nicely though, staring up at me with bulging eyes.

"You're a dirty fucking fighter," he said. He eyed the baseball bat at my feet but didn't go for it. A good sharp shock from my little yellow friend can take most of the *Fuck You* out of a person. "You wanna piece of me then take me on fair."

True enough, but it didn't bother me much. I don't fight fair. If I was a fair fighter I'd be dead by now.

"Laurence Gerbert," I reminded him. "Where is he?"

"Fuck that fucking fucker," he said. "Larry Gerbert's a piece of shit. Let a guy crash here for a while and how does he repay me? Beats me up and takes my … merchandise. Another fucking dirty fighter!"

"Suppose you'd like to see him get pinched?"

My squirming junkie friend stopped in mid whine and began to grin.

"You're fucking A I would."

And just like that I was his best friend.

It's funny, the people you'll work with when you've got a common goal.

He told me everything I needed, and more than I could have expected.

"Richard Dickie?" I asked, just to be certain.

"Yep." My new best friend, a man with the unlikely name of Greaser Gill, sat on a kitchen chair massaging the small burn I'd put on his scrawny chest. "He's calling himself Jim Bose now but I know the *Big Dickie* when I see him."

Richard Dickie, brother of Roy Dickie, the Redwolf accomplice I'd killed years ago. Richard was my final lead in the hunt for Redwolf, the sick fuck who butchered my wife and daughter years before. The same sick fuck had snatched Special Agent Gina White, but she'd escaped and provided the evidence that exonerated me, the only suspect at the time, and doomed Roy Dickie. I'd caught up with Roy, but Richard had vanished so effectively that not even Gina, with all of the federal government's tools at her disposal, had found him.

"How is Dickie involved?" I leaned down over Greaser, repressing the urge to bounce him around his nasty little kitchen like a pinball.

He seemed to be catching a violent vibe from me and stilled in his chair. He looked like he wanted to make himself scarce but couldn't decide which way to run.

I forced myself to back up a step and tried on what I hoped was a reassuring smile. I don't think it was all that comforting, but the extra few feet I'd put between us relaxed him a little.

"Big Dickie comes into town every week or so with a new load of glass … helps me keep the tweakers happy." His face flushed with fresh anger. "Then he recruited that fucktard Gerbert. Mother fuckers jumped me and took my stash! Tryin' to cut me out!"

Greaser indicated the swollen eye and the fresh bruises surrounding it.

Great. My current assignment and shitbag numero uno on my personal hit list were in business together.

"Where are they now?"

Greaser Gill told me.

"Hey, you didn't hear this from me, capiche?" His manic good cheer at seeing an ex-partner-in-crime get fucked evaporated. He seemed to feel he'd said too much and was now eager to insulate himself. "I don't know shit, I didn't say shit, you never fucking saw me!"

"Consider yourself my new confidential informant," I said, and made myself scarce.

ABOUT BRIAN KNIGHT

Brian Knight lives in Washington State with his wife and the voices in his head. He has published over a dozen novels, novellas, and collections in the horror, fantasy, and crime genres.

Subscribe to Brian Knight's Knightmares newsletter for news, updates, and free fiction at www.brian-knight.com.